Dedication

TO ALL WHO

- Have learned—*and those who will*—that rescued animals rescue our souls.

- Establish and run rescue organizations like the Helen Woodward Animal Center.

- Volunteer time and love to rescues; you allow the work to go on.

TO CHILDREN WHO

- Know animals talk.

- Soak up their wisdom.

- Honor each one's uniqueness.

- Understand kindness means both giving *and* receiving.

- Know everything in the world is connected.

May you keep and cherish these gifts your entire lives.

Acknowledgements

Every person named in the book -
you are Rootbeer and Edward's support team.

Helen Woodward Animal Center • **www.animalcenter.org**
The Helen Woodward Animal Center connects people and
animals through many programs, including **Pet Encounter
Therapy**.
PET provides a path for Rootbeer, Edward, dogs, and other
animals to share their magical ability and bring smiles and joy to
people of all ages.

Inspirers & Guides

Candace Conradi	•	www.candaceconradi.com
Olga Singer	•	www.simply-two.com
Gina Dodge	•	www.ginadodge.com
Charlene Edge	•	www.charleneedge.com
Peter Bowerman	•	www.titletailor.com

*Mom, aka Lilly, and all the horse lovers and talented trainers
I am fortunate to know.*

Readers & Encouragers
Mary Lee Howe, Shar Jorgensen, Barbara Edwards, Ali Abercromby
& Kasey Abercromby.

Special Thanks
To Tori, who demonstrated the power of connection between
a little girl and little horses.

A portion of the proceeds from the sale of this book
will go the Helen Woodward Animal Center and
miniature horse therapy and rescue organizations.

Mini Horses, Mighty Hearts

Rootbeer & Edward

Rootbeer
& Edward

First Edition
Copyright © 2019 by Rene Townsend

O'Barke
P R E S S

Encinitas, California

This is a work of fiction. However, first names of characters (except Lilly),
the Helen Woodward Animal Center, and Pet Encounter Therapy are
actual people, places and programs. The events are fictionalized versions
of the actual experiences of Rootbeer, Edward, and the author. Other
resemblance to actual persons, living or dead, is purely coincidental.

Library of Congress Cataloging-in-Publication Data
Townsend, Rene
Mini Horses, Mighty Hearts / by Rene Townsend;
illustrated by Gina Dodge
Summary: Two miniature horses change families, face new, sometimes
scary experiences, meet diverse people and animals,
and find the joy of serving others.

ISBN - 978-1-7322668-0-3
1. Horse - Juvenile fiction. 2. Animals - Juvenile fiction.
3. Values & Virtues - Juvenile fiction.

Illustrator: Gina Dodge
Graphic Designer: Olga Singer

Website: rootbeerandedward.com
Email: rootbeerandedward@gmail.com

Printed in the United States of America

Mini Horses, Mighty Hearts

Rootbeer & Edward

Written by

Rene Townsend

Illustrated by

Gina Dodge

O'Barke
PRESS

Table of Contents

Happy Life

"Edward, would you stop running around and whinnying? I'm just waking up." Through a yawn, I added, "Seriously, you'd think the barn was burning down!"

The sound of the tractor, pulling the wagon with the sweet-smelling hay early in the morning, makes all the horses neigh with delight, including us. Every horse gets excited at mealtime, but I'm pretty sure my brother, Edward, loves food more than any horse at our ranch.

Don't get me wrong—I love food too, but Edward is over the top! When the hay is dropped in our corral, he goes at it like it may be his last meal.

"Food is to be savored, Edward. You're gobbling your food. Slow down, savor the hay—smell the comforting aroma, taste each scrumptious bite, listen to the satisfying crunch."

So much for that advice. When I looked over, I noticed that his hay pile was almost gone, and he was already eyeing my food. Does he chew or simply inhale his food?

"Are you going to eat that little pile there?" Edward asked. "I would really, really like it."

As usual, I pushed a bit of hay over to him. Even though he is a pest, that little black horse is just so darn cute I can't resist. From what I hear, a lot of brothers and sisters are just like Edward—pests.

Edward and I have a person, a human named Katie, who makes sure we have this yummy food and live at a ranch where we are kept safe and healthy. She is just the best and very enthusiastic. For example, Katie loves describing how we became a family and does so with gusto to anyone who asks. Each time, she tells it like she is talking directly to me.

"I always wanted a miniature horse friend, so I went to a ranch where lots of minis live. It was love at first sight. When I saw you, an adorable little, spotted, black-and-white two-month-old foal standing by your mom, I turned to the ranch owner and said, 'I simply have to adopt that one!' That was you, my sweet Rootbeer.

"You were too young to leave your mom that day. I visited you often, so we could get to know each other better. Four months later, when you were six months old, I came  back with my brand new mini horse trailer to take you home to live with me. I was so happy. Really, Rootbeer, you can't imagine how excited I was. All I could do was smile and laugh, thinking of the fun ahead of us."

Katie seemed super nice, but leaving my mom was scary and sad. I whinnied and paced, looking for her day after day. Katie spent lots of time with me, promising to take as good care of me as my mom did, but I missed her. I longed for her warmth, her milk, and even her nips when I got too wild.

For the first few weeks of life, my mom ran alongside me wherever I went. As time went by, she let me roam farther away from her, but she always had an eye on me, even when she was grazing. A quick, sharp whinny from her brought me back to her side immediately.

"You're getting more grown up and independent," she said, "but you must stay where I can see that you're safe."

Until Katie adopted me when I was six months old, I didn't know that almost all horses leave their moms. Often, they are moved to pastures with other horses their age or are adopted by humans. Katie doesn't say she's my human; rather, she is my person, and we are partners. We have been partners for fourteen years.

When I was ten years old Katie said, "Rootbeer, it's time we expand our family. I think you would do well with a mini horse brother."

Here is Katie's second favorite story.

"I searched and searched and finally found Edward," Katie explained. "Like when I first saw you, Rootbeer, I fell in love with this little guy, and knew you would love your new brother too.

"He is registered with the American Miniature Horse Association." I had no idea what "registered" meant, but it sounded impressive.

"His registered name is Royalty's Full of Pizzazz, but people called him Eddy," she continued. "He looked too elegant to be Eddy, so I called him Edward."

Katie was right. The moment I saw him, I knew it would be great to have a brother. It's still true 97% of the time. That was just four years ago, but I can't remember life without my brother Edward by my side. We are inseparable.

Edward is fifteen (one year older than me), but he's smaller and I'm bossier, so everyone considers him my "little brother." To be honest, that sometimes annoys Edward.

Something that annoys both of us is people calling us ponies and asking if we really are horses. We are not ponies. We are horses, only smaller. We're miniature versions of big horses.

"Big or little or in-between, all sizes are just right," Katie tells us. "You two are perfect for me."

Besides, Edward thinks he's the biggest horse anywhere.

"I like that we are unique at our ranch," Edward said. "Only a few of us are miniatures living among lots and lots of big horses. How many do you think live here? Like a hundred or maybe a thousand or a million, zillion?"

"No idea, Edward. The rest of the horses are big— some are enormous. Like us, they have special people who love them and ride them. I am glad we're too little to be ridden."

All the horses at our ranch, whatever their size, have their own homes, individual spaces where they live. These are either a corral outdoors or a stall inside the barn. Even though we're miniature horses, our corral is the same size as the ones big horses live in. Edward and I are in the same corral together, with a huge horse in a corral on each side.

"I wish I could see the horses on each side of us, Rootbeer," Edward said. "These six-foot-high wooden walls let us hear, but not see them. At least we can see out the front and back through these steel railings."

"The humans want each horse to be safe," I said.

"You know how upset and cranky the horses on each side of us can be. The walls keep us safe."

"Still, Rootbeer," Edward went on, "most horses are good-natured. The ones on each side of us like people, but don't seem to like other horses, except maybe us. I know when they get irritated, they try to kick or bite, and we're well protected. I guess the walls are a good thing."

I must admit, there are times when Edward and I bug each other, and sometimes I have to remind my "little brother" to stop being so annoying. I'll make a confession: sometimes I nip at Edward to get him to stop pestering me, but I never hurt him.

Looking out the front or back of our corral is wonderful, as the view changes throughout the day and especially from season to season. Often, I say to Edward, "Stop eating for a moment and look at the heron in the creek," or "Look, a van is bringing a new horse to live here."

When Edward stops eating long enough to look, he is amazed and peppers me with questions: "Where does the heron live when he's not here? How many horses do you think can fit in that trailer? Where are the people taking the horses?" I answer him the best I can, but sometimes I am awake in the middle of the night thinking of answers.

Many horses at our barn compete in horse shows, in events the people call dressage or hunter/jumper shows. We know when it's show time because after the horses get baths, the humans won't let them roll in the dirt. They dry, then groom these show horses and dress them up with fancy halters and pads for their legs and even their heads so they don't get hurt in the trailer.

When Edward hears a big rumble, he says, "Rootbeer, one of those giant horse trailers must be coming to pick up the show horses. I wonder where they are going."

"I don't know, but I heard them saying they'd see their horse friends from other ranches. When they come home with blue, red, and white ribbons, the trainers hang them up on the wall, so I guess it's a big deal."

"It might be fun," Edward said. "But, I wouldn't want to have all those baths and not be able to roll in the dirt."

Our ranch is often busy with activities, but it's also quiet—usually late afternoon and through the night until the morning and the workers arrive. My favorite time is the cool evening just before dark, and all the horses are munching hay contentedly.

"Isn't this the perfect time of day, Edward?"

"It's good," he answers, "but morning is my favorite time."

"I know why. It's because you've eaten all your hay and know the tractor and hay wagon will come soon."

"Want to know a sound I love hearing in the morning, Rootbeer?" Without waiting for an answer, he says, "When the men call out my three favorite words— Bermuda, Timothy, alfalfa. I know we get Timothy hay because it's the best kind for us. Still it's funny for hay to have a boy's name, but I love that the men bring it to us three times a day."

Shaking my head, I turn to look out the back of our corral. Huge leafy trees with multicolored leaves stand among long stretches of grass that are emerald green, thick and luscious. A creek runs past, making gentle, soothing sounds as it flows downhill over rocks. At dawn and early in the evening, birds come to eat big fat bugs and worms. They must think they are delicious, but yuck! They can have all they want. We are vegetarians, and we love grass and hay and the occasional carrot and apple treats. Yum.

"Isn't it beautiful, Edward?"

"It is," he said, "but I can think of an improvement. I'd put our corral in the middle of that grass, so we could eat all the time."

The view out the front of our corral is different. About ten feet away across the dirt aisle are corrals like ours, full of big horses. Behind those corrals is a barn where more horses live, and behind that even more corrals.

We're lucky to live outside because we can see more than horses in the barn can. Outside is lighter and brighter, and people and horses come and go all day long. Tractors rumble past, people push wheelbarrows up and down the rows, veterinarians arrive in their trucks full of medicines, and horse vans go by.

Sometimes we go for an hour to one of the bigger open corrals to play and stretch our legs. All the horses take turns doing this. Big horses go to arenas where they and their riders practice for shows. Other horses and riders go out on miles of trails; we get to walk on these trails. There is so much to see, hear, smell, and do!

The workmen put our hay under the roof that covers

the front part of our corral, where the gate is. We can eat without sun or rain on us, but we like standing in the sun or rain, so we have options. Sometimes we, especially Edward, enjoy standing in the rain, letting it run off our coats.

"Rootbeer, come out here. The rain is soft and refreshing."

Feeling responsible, I'll say, "Edward, come under the cover. You'll get soaking wet, and you might catch cold."

"No, I won't. My hair is so long and thick I won't even feel the cold."

He's probably right, but still ... When fall arrives and the daylight hours become shorter, our hair grows longer and thicker to keep us warm when it's cold or raining. The water runs off unless we stay out too long and get soaked. When rain or cold weather is predicted, Katie puts cozy little blue raincoats on us. See why we love this place and our Katie?

Life was perfect—until it changed.

2

Uncertainty

We like routines. They suit us, and Katie is predictable. Well, until now.

The unknown troubles me. The very idea of change makes me edgy. Of course, we've had changes in our lives, including moving to different barns and pastures. Coming to this barn from a different state was a huge deal. It turned out fine, but it was nerve-racking.

Through all our changes we came to trust Katie, who loves, loves, loves us. And we love, love, love her. We thought all the changes were behind us and we'd enjoy our routine life here—with Katie's smiles, songs, and special treats—forever.

Then Katie started coming to the barn with tears in her eyes. We knew she was going through a tough time and she felt bad. That made me feel bad, too.

"Edward, Katie isn't as happy as usual, so please be extra cute and nice, okay?"

"Of course," he said. "But why is she unhappy? Did we do something to upset her?"

"Nothing I can remember. I suggest we try to make her smile and get her to sing us a song."

Even with all our sweetness, Katie was sad. With tears in her eyes, she made statements like, "What will I do without you boys?" and "Don't worry, you will be just fine." In our minds, those two sentences do not go together.

It got worse. Katie came to the barn less often and for shorter periods of time, leaving with tears in her eyes and causing Edward to ask me, "What's wrong? You've known Katie your whole life. You must know what's happening."

"Everything will be okay, little brother. She'll snap out of it when her tough time is over and be her usual self again."

Although my words sounded reassuring, inside I

wasn't sure everything would be okay. I'll admit it: I'm a worrier, and I was worried.

"You say you aren't worried, Rootbeer, but I can tell you are," said Edward. "When you're worried, you stand still like a statue and stare straight ahead. You're doing that a lot these days."

I thought I'd been hiding my feelings, but Edward saw right through me. He often seems like he isn't paying attention, but he must be. Like all horses, he's sensitive, so faking it never works.

"Yes," I admitted, "I am kind of concerned, but Katie always comes through for us, and she will again." Making that bold statement didn't stop my worrying.

Life at the barn continued to be peaceful. Every day we hoped to see Katie, but we rarely did. Owners of big horses stopped by our corral to say, "Hi. How are you guys?" They petted us through the corral bars, said how much they liked that we live at this ranch, and commented on Edward's beautiful black coat and long, thick mane and tail.

Some quickly reassured me, "You are handsome too, Rootbeer."

It's kind of them to say so, but I'm not as shiny as Edward. My multi-colored coat is black with white spots mixed with a little brown hair, and my mane and tail are not as thick or as long as his. Actually, most of my mane stands straight up. It's kind of unruly, like some kids' hair when they first get out of bed or don't use a comb.

One day, two people stood outside our corral talking about me. One said, "His mane looks frothy. Do you think Katie named him Rootbeer because he reminded her of the frothy top of a root beer float? I loved those as a kid."

"Root beer floats are so delicious," her friend replied. "Why don't we get one someday?"

They were right. Sometimes when Katie tells my adoption story she adds the part about how she named me. "With your soft, fluffy, multi-colored mane, you look like a root beer float. You are as sweet as one, so that will be your name—Rootbeer—and it will be one word, not two."

I don't know what a root beer float is, but I hope I get to taste one someday. It is my namesake, after all.

People said many kind things, but what we noticed most was that every person smiled when they saw us. Those smiles made us happy even though we continued to wonder about our uncertain future.

As the days went on, we saw less and less of Katie, and I became even more stoic. Just as Edward said, I was like a statue, and frankly, Edward's behavior deteriorated. When he's really worried, Edward gets wound up and spins around in the corral like a top. He ran around whinnying and headbutting me and the people who came in to clean our corral.

"That is so annoying, Edward! No one is going to think you're cute if you keep that up." He couldn't help himself and ran around while I stood stock-still.

A lady named Lilly comes to the ranch every day to walk or ride or take care of her horse Kiefer. He lives in the corral across the dirt aisle from us. Without fail, she smiles and talks to us. Sometimes she comes into our corral and scratches us in our favorite spots. I don't know how she knows the best places to scratch, but she does. Maybe Kiefer showed her.

We miss Katie talking to us, so we like that Lilly greets us and tells us stuff.

"Good morning, gentlemen," she said one day. "Katie told me it's okay to come inside your corral whenever I want. I like to do that because you are so special and always make me happy."

That was nice and made us feel a little better.

"Lilly said she talked to Katie," Edward said. "I wish she would tell us more about why Katie isn't coming here."

"I agree, my dear brother, but maybe Lilly doesn't know. Let's try to be content that Lilly sees us every day and tries to make us less worried."

One day, as usual, Lilly walked by and said, "Hi, my little friends." She went to bring Kiefer out of his corral, and we thought she'd go brush him before saddling up to ride. Instead, she brought Kiefer over to our corral and introduced us. She said, "Kiefer, this is Rootbeer and Edward. Edward and Rootbeer, this is Kiefer."

Kiefer is big but not huge like some of the horses around here that are ginormous. Still, Kiefer is about two times taller and three times heavier than we are.

He was curious about us, and wanted to sniff and touch noses, the way horses greet and get to know each other. We wanted to touch noses too, but Lilly said, "That's close enough for today. We'll do this again tomorrow and get closer."

Even though the corral separated us, so all three of us were safe, Lilly said it would be better to meet little by little. Edward and I laughed because we knew we were "little and little."

Over the next couple of days, Lilly brought Kiefer closer and closer until, one day, we touched noses, and we were friends.

"I'd love to see you two little guys and Kiefer play together in a big corral," Lilly said, "but you smaller ones might get hurt playing with a big horse."

It's true: horses can play rough. Maybe that's why we heard Katie tell her kids not to "horseplay."

"Kiefer and Lilly make me happy," Edward said. "But where is Katie? I'm sad she doesn't come to see us."

I nodded my head in agreement and sighed deeply.

I didn't say what I really thought. Seeing Katie sad when she did come made me sadder and even more worried than when we didn't see her. It's awful to see someone you love so unhappy. My thoughts made me restless and unable to sleep that night.

Why is she sad? What's going on with her? *What will happen to us?*

3

Big Change

"Hey, Rootbeer, here comes Katie!" Edward said.

What we hoped would be a happy reunion and a return to the old, normal days, quickly became strange, even eerily foreboding.

Nothing was normal.

Katie came into our corral, took out her cell phone, and started taking pictures. First, she took pictures of me, then Edward, then the two of us together, and finally, some of her with each of us. She smiled during this photo session, then turned away from us and blew her nose.

When she turned back to us, she wasn't smiling. Tears

spilled down her cheeks. Her sad face broke my heart.

Edward was alarmed. "What's wrong with Katie? Have you ever seen her like this?"

"No, Edward, I haven't. I don't know what to say." I stood there looking at Katie and wondering what I could do.

The next thing Katie did was hug Edward and cry into his long, thick black mane, soaking it with her tears. Then she pulled me over to her other side and hugged me too.

"I love you sooooo much. You are my special babies, and you always will be, no matter what," she said.

Suddenly, she jumped up, ran out of our corral, slammed the gate closed, got into her car, and drove off.

The two of us didn't move and stared at the dust cloud billowing behind her car.

Before I could ask Edward if he thought Katie was sick, he hit me with a barrage of questions. "Did we do something wrong? What does 'no matter what' mean? Will she come back? Did she leave forever? What is happening to her? What will happen to us?"

I didn't have a good answer for even one of his questions, especially since I had the very same ones. The best I could do was shake my head and say, "Please try not to worry, Edward. Katie never lets us down. We can count on her to do what is best."

In my heart, though, I wondered if what I'd said was true. Who would take care of us? Horses who live in the wild don't need people, but ones like us—horses who live in barns, corrals, and pastures—do.

You can imagine how scared and sad we were that night. Edward stood with his head down, not wiggling or even eating. I couldn't eat, either. Our corral was strangely silent all night as we huddled together, worrying and wondering what would happen next.

The sun rose and set many times, and the hay wagon

came on its usual schedule, but we didn't see Katie. Neither of us talked about it, but I think we were both afraid she wasn't coming back.

Early one cool morning, Lilly stood near our corral talking to her horse trainer, Debbie. Lilly was scratching Kiefer's neck when Debbie said, "Lilly, you and Kiefer are becoming a good team. You're getting better at giving Kiefer signals he understands using your arms, legs, and the weight and balance of your body. I love seeing your progress together."

"Thanks," Lilly said with a smile. "I appreciate your coaching, and I bet Kiefer does, too.

"There's something I'd like to discuss with you, Debbie," Lilly continued. "It's about Rootbeer and Edward. You told me you have some people in mind who might take them."

I had been munching hay and half listening, but now I froze.

What? Take us? Maybe Katie wasn't coming back. Why? Who? Where? I had a million questions and trembled with anxiety.

Edward must have been listening too because his

head popped up from his hay pile and he started running around in our corral.

My nerves were shot. "Edward, stop! I can't hear what they're saying."

"Yes," Debbie said. "It's so sad that Katie has to move to another state and can't take these two beautiful friends of hers. After she asked me to see if I could find someone who'd give them a good home, I came up with a few possibilities. I plan to call them tonight."

That sent Edward running again until I nipped at him to make him quit.

Lilly and Debbie stood there quietly, looking at us.

"I've been mulling this over for the past week, making a list of the pros and cons of adopting them," Lilly said. "First on my list is that they make me happy. Every time I see them, I smile and feel better about the day, so I'm thinking about adopting them."

"Really? Are you sure?" asked Debbie.

"I think so. They could stay together where they are across from Kiefer. I can try it, and if it doesn't work out, we can look for another person to take them."

We wished we could shout "Yes!" in human talk, but

all we could do was try to be calm, sweet, and extra cute. Edward couldn't stand still any longer and nodded his head up and down while pawing the ground. Lilly and Debbie laughed.

"I think Edward likes that idea," Debbie said.

"Well, I could make a long list of pros," I said to Edward. "We know Lilly, and we like her. She always greets us with a smile, talks to us, and gives us scratches."

Edward chimed in, "And we can stay here in our corral with Kiefer nearby as our special big horse friend. If we can't have Katie, I want Lilly."

"Okay, Edward. We must do everything we can to make Lilly happy that she made this decision and will keep us forever. We don't want her or Debbie looking for someone we don't know to take us who knows where."

"I promise to do my very, very best," Edward agreed.

"Debbie, please text Katie's cell number to me. I'll call her this afternoon," Lilly said. Debbie did it immediately, and they both smiled.

"Look," Edward said. "Lilly has a huge smile on her face. That's a good sign, right?"

Lilly came into our corral. She petted and hugged

us and said, "Do you think you'd like me to take care of you?" We just snuggled up to her and nuzzled her fingers, hoping she'd know that meant "Yes!"

"I could stay here all day with you, but I need to go call Katie and ask her if I can adopt you. See you soon, my little friends."

Edward looked at me and asked, "What now?"

"We wait and see—and hope."

We waited, and waited, and waited. Maybe it wasn't very long, but it seemed like forever before Lilly came back.

"Well, little men, we're now partners."

Edward started running around in circles and neighing. I nickered softly, in my own reserved way. I tried to nuzzle Lilly's hand through the corral. Sensing our need for reassurance, she stepped into the corral.

"Gentlemen, I have an important message for you from Katie," Lilly said. "She is sure you worried when she didn't come to see you. I agreed that you probably were worried, but I told her that I've been talking to you and giving you scratches every day. That made her happy.

"Katie wants you to know that she loves you tons and

tons, but she has to move away and can't take you to her new home. Leaving you makes her terribly sad, but when I promised to love you like she does, she felt better.

"She is happy for us, but she can't bear to come to say goodbye. She asked me to give each of you a hug and a kiss and the message that she will love you forever and ever. Someday I will send her pictures of you, but not for a while, because now it would make her cry. I hope you understand."

We nuzzled her some more, trying to show that we sort of understood. We felt bad for Katie, but we were relieved for ourselves.

"Lilly seems to understand us. Don't you think so, Rootbeer?"

"I do. She seems to speak horse."

"Now our family will be you two, Kiefer, and me," Lilly continued. "I'll come every day to make sure you have what you need and to feed you your extra grain. We'll go for a walk, or I'll take you to a big corral to play. It will be almost like it always was.

"I hope you'll learn to trust me like you trust Katie. Most things will remain the same."

"Ah, Rootbeer," said Edward. "What does she mean by 'most things'?"

Before I could tell him that I didn't know, Lilly said, "Manners. You two are wonderful, and you can be even more wonderful if we improve your manners a bit. Debbie will give us tips on how to be great partners, like she does with Kiefer and me."

"Whoa! What? What are manners?" Edward asked me. "She wants to change us? How? Maybe this won't be as easy as we thought."

"Edward, we have to keep Lilly happy. For now, just relax—and eat."

4

Habits & Manners

"Rootbeer, I'm worried about what Lilly said when she told us we were great but needed to improve our manners," Edward said.

"I'm not sure what is involved, little brother," I responded, "but she said Debbie would help her like she does with Kiefer. He seems happy, so it can't be that bad."

"I know, but I like to do what I like to do, and I don't want to change," Edward said.

Lilly came into our corral, gave us scratches, and said, "I'm so happy to see you. Let's get started on a little training to help us be better partners. Edward, you and I will start, then it will be Rootbeer's turn. I think you're going to like this."

"Humph. I'm not sure what manners are, but I know I don't like to change, or need to change so I have to let Lilly know it." With that, Edward pushed his head into Lilly's leg.

I don't know how hard he pushed, but Lilly said, "Ouch! That is one behavior you must change, Edward. No one likes being bumped, even by a cute little horse. That's like the school yard bully. No one likes a bully and it is not the way to get attention.

"Goats butt objects with their heads, but you are not a goat, and you simply cannot do that. You are a horse, and horses may not behave like that. You weigh over 150 pounds so using your head to bump could bruise a person or even knock them over, especially a child or an elderly person. Headbutting is terrible manners, and you must have good manners." She spoke softly but sternly. We knew she was serious.

"Well, Edward," I said, "now we know Lilly's opinion about one example of manners, and we haven't left the corral yet."

"She can't expect me to stop butting into people," he said. "Lilly said I don't have to get attention that way, but it works. I've always done it, and no one said anything—including Katie, who seemed to think it was cute. Does Lilly think I'll stop just because she gave me a lecture?"

"I'm sure you'll find out, because she is about to halter you."

Lilly led Edward out of the corral. Before they went very far, I heard Edward say, "Ouch!" Soon they were out of sight, but I heard "Ouch!" a few more times.

When they came back, Lilly took off his halter, smiled, and said, "See you later, my friends."

Edward walked straight to the back of the corral, hung his head, and just stood there.

"Edward, what happened? Lilly was smiling and didn't seem upset when she left, but I kept hearing you say 'Ouch!' Did she hit you?"

"Oh, no," he said, "but every time I started to headbutt her, it seemed her elbow or knee was there, and my head ran into it. I said 'Ouch!' because it hurt."

"So, did you learn anything?" I asked.

"Hmmm." Edward stood quietly for a minute, then said, "Since my head hit something hard whenever I pushed into her or butted her with my head, I just hurt myself. Headbutting isn't working with her, so maybe I should try to stop. When I think about it, I guess I hurt other people with my headbutting, just like Lilly said. That makes me feel bad."

I walked closer, nuzzling my little brother to try to cheer him up.

"It's probably good you learned that," I told him. "You are a thoughtful guy and now you know how to be kinder. We know for sure that Lilly will appreciate the change."

A couple of days later, Edward came back from a walk with Lilly and Debbie.

"Changing is hard, Rootbeer," he said. "As we walked along, a couple times I forgot and tried to push into them, but my head hit Debbie or Lilly's knee.

"At the end of our walk, they both praised me, saying I was doing better. Debbie reminded Lilly that habits are hard to change, so practice and consistency are the keys. I think I better break this habit because frankly, I have a bit of a headache.

"But, Rootbeer, do I have to stop butting you too? I mean, it's how I let you know I want to play."

"Maybe it's okay for us," I said. "However, since people don't like it, you better stick to doing it to me only. You know, sometimes it annoys me too, especially when I'm trying to reach that bit of grass outside the fence, just a nose away."

Edward worked extremely hard to stop headbutting— except with me. When he started to push and caught himself, he earned immediate praise from Lilly.

"Thanks for making such an effort to change. You are a fast learner and I'm proud of you," she said, rewarding him with a smile and a scratch.

You may be wondering about the word "scratch." When a human gives a good scratch, it is almost as good as a carrot treat. Lilly knows how and where to give the best scratches. She rubs firmly with her fingertips, not lightly like a fly landing, which is yucky. Horses' favorite spots are our ears, backs, bellies, and the tops of our back legs—places we can't reach to scratch ourselves. Scratching me in those spots makes me close my eyes and sigh with pleasure.

"Good morning, gentlemen," Lilly said. "Time for some new, fun learning. Today we're going to perfect how we help each other put on your halters. We are partners. Cooperating with each other is the best way to begin our time each day."

When I heard Edward sigh, I turned to him and said, "We want Lilly to keep being our partner, right?" I asked him.

He nodded his agreement, bobbing his head up and down with all his might.

"Then let's pay attention and do exactly what she asks." So he did, even though it meant he couldn't keep eating or running around.

"This is very important, gentlemen, because every time you leave the corral, you must wear your halters," Lilly explained. "We halter before we go to big corrals to play, or go for walks, or go to the area where the farriers trim your hooves, or when the veterinarian checks you over. It's a job that horses and humans do together a lot, so let's get it down like pros."

Edward's halter is bright red. It looks great on his little black head, but then everything looks sharp on an all-black horse. My halter is purple. It doesn't show up as much on my black-and-white "frothy" head, but Lilly says I look handsome in it.

Lilly walked up to Edward and put her hand under his chin, lifting his head from the hay. Looking in his eyes, she said, "Here is what I'd like. When I come in to halter you, please stop eating, and stand still with your head up. I'll hold the halter down in front of you, so you can drop your nose into the noseband. That way I can put the top strap over your head and behind your ears and buckle it on the side. The lead rope is always attached so we'll be ready to go out of the corral."

That Edward. He did exactly what Lilly asked. I followed his example, receiving praise.

Learning to halter like this is easy because we like going out. Still, sometimes Edward can't resist trying to grab a bite of hay on the way out. I confess that I do too when there is a tasty morsel within snagging distance.

"Okay," Lilly said. "Rootbeer, since you have the hang of haltering, the two of us are going out to practice walking together.

"When we are walking somewhere, I expect you to walk

next to me, not run ahead or drag along behind," Lilly said.

I guess I didn't listen very well because I ran ahead of her. Immediately, I felt a tug on the lead rope that put pressure on my nose and poll, which is a sensitive area on the top of my head where the halter fits behind my ears.

"Rootbeer," she said. "Come back here, my good fellow."

As soon as I returned to her side, Lilly let the lead rope hang down loosely between us.

"See how great that feels when you're next to me, Rootbeer? I'll bet you don't feel any pressure."

I bobbed my head in agreement. I felt free, like I was walking without a halter and we were just two friends out for a nice stroll. When Lilly reached down and scratched my ears, I sighed my thanks. Ear scratches feel so good that it makes me wonder why humans don't scratch each other's ears.

When I got back, Edward peppered me with questions.

"What did you do? What did you learn? Did it hurt? Is it hard to do what Lilly wants?"

"Whoa, Edward. It's super easy. Just walk next to Lilly at her pace, and you'll have a great, peaceful walk. And do not bump her with your head."

"That's it?"

"Yup. You don't like pressure any more than other horses, so just do what she asks. It's that simple. You'll feel no pressure, and best of all, it makes Lilly happy."

"And she'll keep us?" Edward asked.

"I am confident she will," I told him. "She has Kiefer and now us. I think she's happy with all three of us. Besides, I heard her tell Debbie that although we occasionally slip up on our new manners, we're doing great. She laughed and said she sometimes forgets her manners too."

Edward sighed contentedly—and lowered his head into the hay pile.

5

Getting Sick

Edward had a horrible, terrible night!

He didn't eat. His head hung down. He kicked at his tummy with his back feet and flopped onto the ground, rolling back and forth. Something was seriously wrong.

"What's the matter, Edward? You seem to be in a lot of pain." I felt panicky.

"My tummy really hurts," he moaned. "It feels like something is stuck inside."

Talk about feeling helpless. I stayed near Edward and tried to think of something I could do to help but couldn't come up with anything. The night lasted forever. I was so relieved when Lilly arrived early in the morning.

She was alarmed at the sight of Edward.

"Little buddy, are you sick? You look awful and haven't touched your hay. Come with me, little man. We are going for a walk while I call Dr. Steve," Lilly said, haltering Edward.

A friend walking her horse heard the commotion and asked, "What's wrong? Can I help?"

"Please. Edward is not doing well. It would be a huge help if you would keep him moving while I call the veterinarian. Thanks."

I moved to the front of our corral while Lilly paced back and forth. She dialed Dr. Steve, listened for a few seconds, and then said, "Emergency!" Dr. Steve must have answered immediately because Lilly told him what was happening.

She described Edward's symptoms and said a friend was walking Edward and preventing him from lying down. "What else should I do? Should you come now?"

She was quiet for a while. I wanted to know what Dr. Steve was saying, but only Lilly could hear him.

"Okay, we'll keep him walking and won't let him roll,"

Lilly said. "Yes, I still have the emergency pain medication you left with me. Please tell me how to give it to him."

Again, she was quiet.

"Let me repeat what you said to be sure I do it the correct way. I give him a double dose of the paste, squirting it in the back of his mouth and holding his head up so he can't spit it out. Then what?" She listened some more.

"Yes, we'll hope that works. I'll call you in an hour if there is no improvement. Thank you. I hope you don't have to come, but thanks for standing by just in case."

Lilly told the friend walking Edward what the doctor had said. By this time, her other friends with horses at our ranch had gathered around. When they saw sad little Edward, they offered to help, and took turns keeping him moving and not letting him roll.

"You're all so great," Lilly said to them. "I love how horse people always jump in to help each other."

All the people had something to do, but I could only stand there watching and calling to Edward every time he walked by. A couple of people stopped to scratch me and tell me it would be okay, but I didn't feel that way.

Lilly ran to her tack trunk to find the medicine. She

returned with a long tube and squirted some white, pasty-looking medicine in the back of Edward's mouth. He was so sick that he didn't even try to resist the disgusting-looking stuff. No matter how much he pulled back to stop or tried to lie down, Lilly's friends kept Edward walking.

"Would you walk Rootbeer next to Edward?" Lilly asked a friend. "It might comfort both of them. The vet hopes the combination of medicine and walking will unstick the blockage in his intestines and get it moving out of him."

"It's awfully hard to see your best friend sick, isn't it?" Lilly asked, giving me a scratch.

I had never thought of him as my best friend, just my brother. I realized that Lilly was right. Edward was my best friend. I liked that, but it made me even more scared. What if he didn't get better?

Just then, Lilly asked my walker for help, so we trotted quickly back to our corral. She unhaltered me and went to help Lilly and Edward.

"Edward is trying hard to lie down," Lilly said. "Please push while I pull to keep him up. Rolling and twisting his intestines will make it worse.

"Come on, fella," she pleaded. "I know you hurt, but I can't let you stop walking, and you certainly can't roll. Keep going, little man."

I whinnied and begged him, too. "Please do what she asks, Edward. She knows best, and she's doing everything to help."

Each time Edward walked by our corral, I asked, "Are you feeling any better at all? Can you talk to me?"

He didn't say anything and continued to look miserable. His head hung so low it almost touched the ground. I felt miserable too!

Then I heard Lilly call Dr. Steve again.

"It doesn't look like the medicine and walking are working. Please come." After a pause she added, "Oh, thanks.

"Edward, Dr. Steve is on his way. Rootbeer, please try not to worry. The doctor is coming."

Even though Lilly's words were comforting, her face had an anxious, worried look.

From down the aisle, a person called, "Hi, Lilly, I'm here."

Lilly had forgotten that she had invited a friend to the

ranch to meet us and Kiefer. When she saw Lilly's look of surprise, her friend said, "Should I have called you? What's going on?"

"Edward is not feeling well, Gloria." Lilly dropped her voice to a whisper. "He may have colic."

"Sounds serious," Gloria said.

"It sure can be," Lilly told her.

They were talking softly, but I could hear everything.

"Horses can't throw up, so food has to go all the way through them. If it gets stuck in their intestines, it really hurts and can be very serious, even deadly. I gave him a paste that, along with walking, often works, but it didn't this time. Only a veterinarian can do the next procedure. Thankfully, Dr. Steve will be here any moment."

"Oh gosh! Anything I can do?" Gloria asked.

"Just hope Dr. Steve can do his magic. I can't imagine life without this little guy."

Gloria reached out and hugged Lilly.

All of us were hopeful when Dr. Steve drove up. He always seems to know exactly what to do.

"Lilly, please bring Edward over here," said Dr. Steve as he grabbed his bag from the truck. "I'll do the procedure in front of their corral so Edward and Rootbeer can see each other. They'll both be less stressed that way."

I don't know about Edward, but it made me feel better that I could see him getting help.

"Okay, buddy," Dr. Steve said. "I'm giving you this relaxation shot before I put this tube in, and then I'll pour in oil to push out whatever is blocking you."

Relaxing, Edward's head dropped a little more and Dr. Steve stuck a long, narrow tube up Edward's nose (ouch!). The tube reached way down into his tummy.

It was hard to watch, but I wanted to see if the tube and oil would work. We waited and waited. I kept telling Edward that he'd get better, but even though he was groggy from the relaxing shot, Edward mumbled, "My tummy still hurts."

After watching and waiting for what felt like a long time, Dr. Steve said gently, "Well, Lilly, I've done all I can with this tube and oil, and he's still blocked. I recommend you take him to the hospital."

Looking worried and sad, Lilly agreed.

"Will you call the hospital and tell them I can have Edward there in an hour? I need to go home, get the trailer, come back, and transport him, and it will take that long."

Oh, dear.

Gloria and another horse friend offered to take care of Edward while she went for the trailer.

As she gathered a few things from the corral, I heard Lilly say to Gloria, "Nothing like having your first real trailer-pulling experience be an emergency. I've only practiced, but now I have to do it, and I will."

This was Lilly's first "real" trailer experience? I was too concerned about Edward to think about it.

Lilly arrived back at the ranch and maneuvered her truck and trailer in front of our corral.

"Do you think Edward will get in?" she asked her friends.

To everyone's surprise, my little brother hopped in. I think he knew the hospital was the best place to get help. What a trooper.

"Oh, Edward," she said. "You're just so great. We'll be at the hospital in just a few minutes.

"The veterinarians and hospital assistants are terrific. They will help Edward get better," Lilly said to me. "Try not to worry."

Not worry? How could I not worry when I saw them drive off with my brother, who was so sick he didn't even call back to me when I whinnied and whinnied to him?

That was the worst night of my life. I was alone without Edward for the first time since Katie adopted him and brought him home. The big horses nickered and whinnied to me, trying to make me feel better and not so alone.

Kiefer stayed at the end of his corral across from ours, watching me. "Thanks, Kiefer," I said. He nickered softly and stayed there all through the night. It wasn't the same as having my brother next to me, but it was kind, and it helped.

"Edward is doing better," Lilly said the next morning as she came into our corral. "He will be fine, but the hospital veterinarian wants him to stay there another day and night to be sure he is 100%."

Another night in the hospital didn't sound fine to me. I wanted to see him for myself.

Lilly, sensing this, tried to reassure me. "I'd take you to see him, but the hospital doesn't allow it. The hospital vet, who is a partner of Dr. Steve's, is the absolute best at colic treatment. We need to trust him and his team, so try to relax." I did, but only a tiny bit.

"Let's go for a short walk," Lilly said. I was happy to get out of the corral and move.

"I'm going to the hospital," Lilly said after our walk. "I'll come back soon and tell you how he's doing. Everyone at the ranch wants to know too."

When she returned, Lilly was smiling. "Edward is definitely better. Before he comes home, we need to make changes to the corral you and Edward share. Tomorrow, my friend Tony and I will install some low corral fencing to divide your space in half. You will be able to touch each other over and through the divider. This remodel will let you be side by side and see each other the same as before—together but separate."

I was so happy Edward was coming home that I didn't care about the remodel. Besides, I loved the attention Lilly was giving me—scratches in the best spots and her soft, reassuring, happy-sounding voice. I was kind of dreaming until I heard her talk about food.

"We need to control Edward's eating to help prevent colic, and we need to fatten you up a bit. You'll get the amount of hay that's just right for you. Edward won't be able to eat your share, and I can give you additional special food that you each need. You'll both be healthier."

After that explanation, being together but separate sounded good. As you know, I like food, but not like Edward, who gobbles food, and then wants mine. Maybe that's what made him get sick, and a little chubby, while I was too thin.

"Let's do a short walk around the ranch," she said.

It turned out to be a long walk because every person stopped us to ask how Edward was doing. Lilly explained and said she expected to bring him home tomorrow. Everyone smiled and said how happy the news made them.

Returning to our corral, Lilly said, "Just one more night alone, Rootbeer. Tony and I will change the corral in the morning, and then we'll go get Edward."

"Sometimes it takes longer to get over colic," Kiefer said, standing at the end of his corral. "Edward fought to get better. He is a tough little guy."

I knew Kiefer was right. That thought, along with Kiefer keeping watch over me that second night and reassuring me, helped me be less worried.

Lilly's smile when she arrived early the next morning had to mean good news.

"The veterinarian called. Edward is ready to come home. We'll fix the corral and go get him."

Tony and Lilly quickly put a white plastic divider with railings down the middle of our space. There was plenty of room for each of us to move around, but Edward would have to be content with running around in only half the area he was used to. I was thinking that this division was a great idea.

"Tony and I are off to get Edward," Lilly said, giving me a few good scratches.

I stood in the corral, ears forward, listening for their return. From a long way off, I heard the truck and the rattle of the trailer getting closer. I knew exactly when Lilly turned into the ranch and I started whinnying. Kiefer and the other big horses joined in to welcome Edward home, bobbing our heads up and down when we heard him call back. We whinnied to each other until Edward got off the trailer, and Lilly walked him into his new half of our corral.

What a great homecoming!

He was surprised by the divider but didn't say anything. After sniffing it, he pushed against it, looked at me, and said, "Hmm, is this thing staying? Is this the way it's going to be from now on?"

"I think so," I said. "I'll explain later. For now, enjoy being home."

"It really wasn't awful at the hospital, but I am happy to be home," he said, reaching over to touch noses.

I looked over at Kiefer and said, "Thanks for being my friend and watching over me. You were right about colic taking time to heal and Edward being a tough guy. I am very grateful for your friendship." Kiefer nickered back and went to eat his breakfast.

When I looked at Edward, his head was buried in a pile of hay. I sighed contentedly and thought, our Edward is healthy again. I sure hope he stays that way.

6

Learning New Stuff

After the scary hospital trip, our lives returned to their normal routines. Adjusting to the divided corral was easy, although Edward complained that he couldn't reach my hay.

"Hey, Rootbeer," he said in his sweetest tone, "since it's nice to share, wouldn't you like to push a little of your hay my way? You may be gaining too much weight."

"Very funny, Edward," I said. "I'm still too skinny, but I must compliment you on your smaller tummy."

"I'm not fat," he retorted.

"I didn't say that. I only said that you look more svelte without the round belly."

"What's that supposed to mean?" Edward said.

"It means this new, slimmer you, is more handsome than ever."

"Well, I don't want to get too svelte, so how about just a tiny bit of that big pile you have?"

That guy—he never gives up. I chuckled and continued dining leisurely.

Every day, we ate hay, had our special food, drank water, played in a big corral, or went on walks with Lilly and sometimes one or more of her people friends. Our favorite visitors were her little people friends, the ones she called "children" or "kids."

"I like that they are our size and we can see eye to eye with them," Edward said.

When newcomers visited, Lilly told them about us, demonstrating how to treat us and take care of us. That's comforting and makes us feel more secure.

"Here's the most important thing to remember," she told the kids.

"Respect Rootbeer and Edward and insist on good manners. They will respect you, and when all living beings respect each other, we get along better and live as friends.

"Here's the safe zone," Lilly said as she stood by our shoulders. "Avoid their bums, but if you're walking around behind them, put a hand on their backs so they know you're there. If something startles horses, they might jump or kick out and hurt someone without meaning to.

"Let me show you how to put on a halter, and then you can do it."

"The kids seem very serious," Edward said. "I like how they listen and watch Lilly carefully and try to do what she does."

"I agree," I said. "Sometimes it takes a few tries to get it right, just like when we're learning something new. Let's stand quietly while they practice."

One of the kids asked, "Can we ride them? They are just our size."

"No," Lilly said. "The minis are too small. Even though you're small too, it could hurt their backs. Maybe a tiny child could ride them, but I don't think that's safe either, so we just walk alongside them."

"I like that she protects us, Rootbeer," Edward said. "We're safe with her."

"Me too. Did you notice that the kids who come often

are getting more confident?"

"Yes," Edward answered. "Reese, Ali, and Kasey put our halters on the right way, they know which combs and brushes to use to clean us, and they walk along beside us like Lilly showed them. Brogan is very young, but he knows the right way to pet us. I like these kind, smart kids."

The next time Ali and Kasey visited, Lilly asked them, "Do you want to vacuum the minis?"

"Vacuum horses?" they said in unison, giggling at the idea. "You mean like mom and dad vacuum the carpets?"

"Yes," Lilly said. "We have a horse vacuum with a hose attachment that professional groomers use to get dirt out of the horses' coats. Do you want to try it?"

The girls continued to giggle and laugh as they vacuumed us. Lilly laughed too, praising the girls for the good job they did. We bobbed our heads because it felt so good.

"People can clean us all they want, but it won't last," Edward said. "I love dirt!"

"We are dirt magnets," I said. "People always laugh when we get up from a roll and shake out a cloud of dust.

They probably don't know how good rolling in the dirt feels on our skin and all over our bodies, or that it helps keep bugs away."

Edward and I were getting used to the changes in our lives, and we like being with Lilly. In fact, we look forward to what she will dream up for us to do next, even when it's a little scary.

"I like walking with Lilly on new paths and trails around the ranch," Edward said. "When we go up and down the aisles of corrals, we get to see the other horses who are lucky to live here too. I like meeting them."

"Some of my favorite times are when Lilly walks us and meets people walking their horses," I said. "It is special when she asks a person if her horse would like to meet us, or when the other person asks if her horse can meet us."

What's really interesting are the different reactions some horses have to us. You will think this is funny, but some of the big horses act afraid of us. Really! Their eyes get big and some back up. Others even squeal, snort, and try to turn away.

To meet them, Lilly walks us step by step toward the

other horse, just like when we met Kiefer. If the big horse seems too nervous, we all stop and agree to come closer another time. Usually, the big horse becomes curious and wants to get closer. Lilly never forces us to meet. After two or three times, we touch noses, and everyone is happy.

The first time Edward squealed meeting a new horse, I asked him, "Big horses sometimes squeal, but why do you?"

"I do it to show I am not afraid and want them to know it!" he said.

You already know that Edward thinks he's a big horse. Being brave comes in all sizes—big, in-between, and little.

One day, Lilly said, "Gentlemen, today you both get to play on the obstacle course Debbie set up for training. The obstacle course is a challenge and reasonable challenges are good for all of us. Rootbeer, you'll be first, and then you, Edward."

"I'm glad you're going first, Rootbeer. You can tell me what a 'reasonable challenge' is as I'm not too sure. The word 'obstacle' makes it sound hard."

"I will let you know, Edward," I said, although I wasn't

too sure about any of it either. As Lilly walked me to the course, she told me what to expect.

"First, we'll walk over the bridge that tips like a small teeter-totter and then you'll learn to step over a series of logs of various sizes and widths. Some are close together, and others are at odd angles. Later, our challenge will be walking up and down two stairs. Kiefer and I have walked and ridden over all of these. It's fun."

We'll see, I thought to myself, *but if Kiefer can do it, at least I can try my best.*

"Patience is the key, Rootbeer," Lilly said. "We will take it step by step and do the best we can on each obstacle. We don't expect perfection the first time, but we will make progress. Remember, patience and practice are the keys to improvement. Learning takes time."

I wanted to tell Lilly I already knew that because we've learned and practiced many new behaviors since we met her. But I focused on what she asked me to do.

Going over all the logs was the easiest. I stepped over them and even jumped a couple. That made Lilly laugh and exclaim, "You are a talented jumper, Rootbeer!"

After we went through all the obstacles a couple of

times, Lilly said, "That's enough for our first session. Now I'll get Edward."

The second I got back to the corral, Edward wanted to know what had happened. As I started to tell him, Lilly haltered him, and off they went.

"The hardest thing for you," I called after him, "will be patience."

I could hardly wait to share our experiences.

The minute he returned, he said, "I went over a couple of logs, but then I figured it was easier to run around the ends. Lilly laughed but said we needed to go back and try it again. Eventually, I went over all of them. Lilly was delighted. I was, too."

"What did you think of the tippy bridge?" I asked him.

"At first, moving up and down was scary, but then I thought it was fun," Edward said. "What about you?"

"I must admit I was nervous on the tippy bridge. But soon, I could step up on it, stand in the middle, and go down the tippy side. I wonder what the stairs will be like."

"I don't know, Rootbeer, but all this learning makes me hungry."

Some things never change.

Every week, Lilly took us through the course until we mastered all of the obstacles. Edward and I agreed that getting good at anything new made us more confident, stronger, and eager for challenges. That's fortunate, because Lilly is forever thinking up some different ones.

She kept expanding our experiences, taking us on new trails and to places with all kinds of enticing sights, sounds, and smells. Edward and I prefer going together, but Lilly said, "I want each of you to have courage and be brave. New experiences are everywhere, and I want you to tackle them without fear, whether you are together or alone. You can do it."

"Lilly sure is enthusiastic," Edward said. "She makes me want to do what she asks, or at least not resist too much."

One day when Lilly took us over the log obstacles together, Edward laughed and said, "Look, Rootbeer. With my svelte self, I can clear all the big logs."

I nickered, making Lilly look down.

"Look at you, Edward. You've lost weight, and now you're trim and sleek," she said. "Your tummy didn't drag on any of the logs. I'm proud of you because it's hard to lose weight."

I could see that Edward was proud of himself, too.

We love to play in the big corral, which we do almost every day. Lilly likes to watch us play, but sometimes she tells us she needs to do chores.

"While you guys are having a grand time, I'll clean your corral. When you come back, you'll have fresh water in your buckets and new shavings, so you can have a great roll and a soft, comfy place to sleep."

Lilly is a good corral keeper. Fresh shavings are especially great for rolling and sleeping. People who don't know about horses ask Lilly if we lie down or stand up to sleep. Want to know a cool fact? We do both. We lie down, but mostly we sleep standing up—something we can do because our back legs can lock so we don't fall down. I wonder if people can sleep standing up.

"Hey, Rootbeer," said Edward. "Next time Lilly takes us to the corral, let's run the minute we get there, then roll, then we'll run around again. The dirt will really stick."

"You are such an imp," I said. "But, if we roll, run, roll and run again we can get the dirt to stick even more."

"Awesome!" Edward replied.

So, we did just that. We rolled in the dirt, chased each other around, nipped each other's legs in a game of tag, then rolled again. We also reared up in pretend battle like horses do in the wild. When we ran out of

breath, we stood still until we stopped gasping for air, and then Edward started it all over again. What a blast!

"When Lilly comes back, I bet she'll roll her eyes, sigh at the mess we are, and laugh anyway," I said. That's just what she did.

Sometimes Lilly rides Kiefer while we play, and at other times he is in a big corral next to us while she cleans his and our corrals. Since we're friends, we always touch noses.

"Wouldn't you like to play our run, nip, and rear games with us, Kiefer?"

"I'd love to, Rootbeer," Kiefer replied, "but you know that Lilly is afraid a nip or even a play kick from me could hurt you. I wouldn't do it on purpose, but you know how rough we all can be. I'll run around my corral, and you run around in yours. It's not the same as being together, but we'll have fun. Then we can all roll and get dirty."

"Life is wonderful, isn't it, Edward?"

7

Mini Play Day

"Hey, my friends," Lilly said early one morning. "Are you ready for a new adventure?"

"Here we go again," Edward said to me.

"It's a Mini Play Day at a park about a thirty-minute drive from here," Lilly continued. "You and about fifty other miniature horses will get to do all kinds of activities. Remember how much fun you had playing with Wanda's four minis when they were here? They are going too."

Wanda is Lilly's new trainer. She and her team take good care of us when Lilly is away.

"What's a Mini Play Day?" Edward asked me.

"Where is it? What will we do? Will we meet other minis? Can we eat there?"

"Egads, Edward! I've never been to a Mini Play Day and have no idea. Lilly always explains, so be patient." I used my best reassuring voice but wasn't all that confident myself. Lilly helps us face challenges, but this sounded big.

"Come on, gentlemen. I'll tell you what I know about the day while we walk to our obstacle course," Lilly said.

"I've been told there will be a variety of contests, including an obstacle course. Some obstacles may be like those you know, but there will be new ones too."

"New ones?" Edward said to me. "Like what?"

I gave him a little nip. "Just listen, please."

Fortunately, Lilly ignored our exchange.

"I heard there will be barrel racing, a jumping course—which you'll love, Rootbeer—a costume contest, a costume parade, and musical towels," Lilly said.

Edward was about to start in again, so I stopped him with "the look" and Lilly continued.

"Musical towels is a game similar to musical chairs kids and adults play. Obviously, horses don't sit in chairs, so instead there will be towels on the ground in a huge circle. Each team of a mini and a person starts out on a towel. Once every team is on a towel, the music starts. While the mini-person teams walk around in a circle to the right, one towel is removed. When the music stops, every team has to run and get at least one hoof on a towel. The rules are only one team per towel, so whoever doesn't reach an open towel is out of the game. This goes on until only one towel is left with two final teams. The music starts for the last time, and the first team to the one towel wins. Sound fun?"

Edward glanced over at me and said, "I'm not sure. It sounds stressful."

I agreed, but Lilly was so enthusiastic that I bobbed my head up and down.

"Wanda, her assistants, and I wracked our brains for days thinking up costume ideas. Finally, we decided the six of you could be a great football team."

"Now that sounds fun," Edward exclaimed.

"Do you know what a football team is?" I asked him.

"No, but I like the team and costume idea," he answered.

Frankly, it sounded silly, but I didn't want to be a spoilsport.

Janet, a friend of Lilly's who rides her horse Snickers with Lilly and Kiefer, walked over to us at the obstacle course. Lilly told her about Mini Play Day and asked if she wanted to be part of the fun.

"You bet. Shall we practice now?" she asked.

"Absolutely," Lilly responded, handing her my lead rope.

I sailed over the jumps, clearing them by a foot. Edward did a couple of low jumps, then decided he could walk over them. I sighed and rolled my eyes at him while Lilly and Janet laughed. We both did the tippy bridge and logs with ease.

"My little friends, there'll be obstacles at Mini Play Day that you've never seen before, so be brave and try your best," Lilly said. "Nothing will hurt you, I promise."

Janet and Lilly returned us to our corral and went to help Wanda's group make costumes.

"I'm confident we can do these contests, Rootbeer," Edward said. "Do you think wearing costumes is like wearing our raincoats?"

"We'll find out soon, little brother."

Sure enough, later that day, Lilly and Janet came to

our corral, smiling and laughing together.

"Hey, guys, want to hear about the costumes?" Janet asked.

I had a sense of dread, and Lilly's description didn't do much to relieve that feeling. Being a rather dignified horse, the idea of any costume sounded bewildering and silly.

"Rootbeer, you and Cody—Wanda's buckskin mini that you've played with—are the biggest, so you will be football players. You'll wear the football jerseys we made, complete with numbers. You are 007, a very famous number!

"Edward, since you're all black, we'll paint white stripes on you, making you the perfect referee. I see you shaking your head, Edward, but don't worry; the paint is washable. The rest of your costume is a referee's hat and a big whistle hanging around your neck."

"Ha," I said to Edward. "Good thing your cap will say 'referee' or you'd look like a zebra."

"Two of the girl minis are cheerleaders, and Sassy, the smallest girl mini with brown hair, will be painted like a football," Janet said.

She and Lilly were having a grand time. I have to say

that Edward and I were good sports to go along with the costume idea when we didn't even know what football players, referees, or cheerleaders do.

Early on Mini Play Day morning, Janet and Lilly put our food, water, treats, and costumes into Lilly's truck and then came to get us. All the buzzing around made me nervous, but Edward was excited. Before we knew it, we were in the trailer and off to our new adventure.

"Holy cow, Edward!" I could hardly believe my eyes. When we arrived at the park and Lilly and Janet brought us out of the trailer, we watched as trailer after trailer drove in and unloaded one, two, or more minis.

"Everywhere I look, there are minis, Edward."

Normally wiggly Edward took in the scene around us, full of curiosity. He seemed calm and relaxed, but I felt a nervous, even hyper, energy building inside me. This was a total role reversal.

Lilly and Janet walked us to where Wanda's group had set up an open-sided tent for sun protection. Her four minis were calm like Edward. Because Edward was so mellow, I think Lilly assumed I was fine, too. She was too busy learning how to register us for the day and figuring out the sequence of events, to notice my anxiety.

"Edward," I said, "aren't you a little nervous? Doesn't this seem kind of scary?"

"Huh?" he replied. "Scary? What's there to be nervous about? Look at all these cool minis and all the colorful ribbons and stuff flapping around in the arena."

He gazed around in amusement, not noticing I was shaky.

When Lilly looked at me, I must have been wild-eyed, because she said, "Why don't we go for a walk, guys? Seeing everything will make you feel better."

As we went around the outside of the arena, Janet

walked Edward, and I was with Lilly.

When the announcer said it was warm-up time, Wanda's assistants came over. One of them asked, "Do you want us to take the guys over the obstacles and jumps?"

"Thanks. That would be terrific," Lilly said.

I felt better moving around, and I loved doing the jumps. Some obstacles looked frightening, though. On one, ribbons dangled from overhead down to where they touched us. Another had foam tubes coming out from both sides of a narrow pathway. I couldn't believe they expected us to walk through those floppy, flapping sticks. The logs and bridges were like the ones at home, but the plastic pool full of water stopped me in my tracks.

Edward went through everything first. After he came back, he said, "All those dangly things tickle, but I liked it all. The water pool is weird but shallow."

He saw my hesitation and asked, "Are you okay? What's wrong?"

"Nothing," I said. I pulled myself up to my full height and took a deep breath. Then I moved forward and went through and over every obstacle, but I wouldn't call it fun. I managed to avoid the pool by running around the side of it, making Edward laugh.

Lilly noticed I still was not my normal self. With all the minis and activity going on, my mind was racing, my body was tensing up, and I didn't feel safe.

"Rootbeer, let's take another walk to see if that will relax you."

I'm sorry to say that it had the opposite effect. As Lilly and I walked off toward an open space, it turned bad. For some reason, I took off running back to the obstacle course—and then it got worse. I ran so fast and out of control that I dragged Lilly down in the dirt! I was shocked at my behavior and skidded to a stop. Edward and Janet ran over, looking very concerned.

While Janet was helping Lilly up and brushing the dirt off her clothes, Edward said, "Rootbeer, what is wrong with you? Why did you do that? You could have hurt Lilly."

Lilly was covered in dust. Fortunately, she wasn't hurt, but I hung my head in shame and sadness. I couldn't believe I acted that way.

"Well, that surprised me," Lilly said. "I expected

Edward to be somewhat anxious, but not you, Rootbeer. I need to think about this."

"Do you think a little trailer time would help to settle them?" Janet asked.

"Good idea," Lilly said.

When we were in the trailer, Edward turned to me and said, "Geez, Rootbeer, I'm the one who usually gets in trouble, but here we are in 'time out' because of you. I've been calm and didn't do anything wrong."

"I'm so sorry, Edward. I feel terrible. I don't know what got into me and made me so overwhelmed and out of control. Lilly and Janet know you didn't do anything wrong. I'm sure the reason you're in here too is to help me get myself together."

"Well, you help me out a lot, so I guess it's my turn to help, Rootbeer. Still, I'd rather be out there having fun."

"I know. I'll do lots better if Lilly gives me another chance."

Once the contests were ready to begin, Lilly and Janet came to get us. I kept my promise. It seems the unfortunate incident woke me up. I focused on a goal and that got my mind and body under control. We did all the events, and I actually enjoyed them almost as much as Edward.

As the day wound down, we walked to the sun shelter for a rest.

"Even though it was all for fun, I love that we got ribbons like the big show horses do," Edward said. "I'm proud of our second place in the costume contest even though I wanted to win first place. The brown minis dressed up like lions did deserve first place. I love your red ribbon for musical towels and your first-place blue ribbon for jumping, Rootbeer."

"I do, too," I said, "but the ribbon for getting second place in musical towels is my favorite ribbon."

"Why not the blue for first place in jumping?" Edward asked.

"We could have won musical towels, but did you see what my partner Carina did? She held me back to let the tiny little girl with the tiny little mini win. That girl just beamed. I'll never forget her smile, so getting second was perfect. Carina did the right thing."

I sensed Lilly coming up. She put her hand on my back and said, "It's been a long day, and we still have a drive ahead of us. Is it okay with you gentlemen if we skip the last contest and go home?"

I nodded my head up and down in agreement.

"Oh, Rootbeer, I'd better be careful," Lilly said. "I think you understand everything I say. I'll bet you do too, Edward. You two are the best."

Wow, was I ever relieved to hear that. I still felt bad, but that relieved my guilt a little, tiny bit.

On the ride home, Edward asked, "What do you think about today, Rootbeer?"

"Well, Edward, I learned a lot. I got too nervous and should have been braver. I certainly wish I hadn't taken off running and made Lilly fall. When she didn't get mad at me, I felt even worse. She said she was sorry I was so stressed. It would have been easier if she'd gotten mad at me.

"What about you, Edward? What did you think?"

"I'm sorry you were anxious, but I'm proud that I wasn't. I didn't like having to go to 'time out' with you, but you help me when I'm in trouble, so it's okay. I was too busy having fun to help you as much as I could have. Maybe we can help each other more in new situations."

We munched hay and were quiet for a long time.

"Let's make a deal, Rootbeer. Next time, we'll tell each other if one of us gets upset or anxious, and we'll ask for help before we lose control, okay?"

"That is a deal, my brother. I promise to do better next time. I'm glad you had such a great day. You're my best pal."

Neither of us remembers being led back to our corral or Lilly saying good night. I'll tell you what—we both slept hard and long that night.

A Job?

Summer drifted into fall. The air cooled, and each day the sun rose later and set earlier, giving us long, dark nights.

My coat was getting thicker, but Edward's...

"You look like a woolly mammoth!" I said. "Horses all over the world get longer, thicker hair in this weather, but you'd win the blue ribbon for both long and thick. Well, you would if there was a contest for that sort of thing."

"Are you making fun of me or are you jealous?" he nickered.

"Maybe a little jealous. You will definitely be nice and toasty through the long, cold winter nights."

One chilly morning Lilly arrived, her breath coming out in foggy blasts. Still, she was chipper.

"Good morning, my friends," she said. "Let's go walk. The autumn leaves are crunchy and colorful all along the ranch trails, even on the wide-open Butterfly Trail."

Playing together in a big corral, "horsing around" with each other, and taking walks with Lilly are our favorite activities, especially when the walks include stopping to graze on lush green grass.

Every few minutes, Lilly stopped, and took deep breaths.

"Look at these colors, gentlemen. Have you ever smelled or seen anything more beautiful? The leaves clinging to the trees are every shade of yellow, orange, and red. Even trees that lost their leaves are gorgeous. We can see the birds more clearly. Shh—listen. The birds are singing to us."

Fidgety Edward kept shuffling his hooves and rustling the leaves, so I gave him a hip check, bumping him with my hindquarters. It's a favorite move of mine when we're playing.

"It's okay, Rootbeer," Lilly said, leaning down to scratch my ears. "The leaves crunching and crackling along with the birds singing is our own symphony. Music for our happy trio."

"Our own symphony," Edward said. "I like that. But what does she mean about reds and oranges and yellows?"

"Good question, Edward. Let me think about it." We continued to walk contentedly next to each other.

"I think humans see colors they call red or orange that we don't see," I said. "They probably have other special colors, but we see the one that matters—green."

"Like over there?" Edward asked. "Think we can get her to take us to inspect, and taste, our favorite color?"

I nickered softly back to the ever-hopeful Edward.

As we strolled and sometimes trotted alongside Lilly, people walking their dogs stopped to talk and compare their dogs' sizes to us. Most are smaller, of course, but we've seen big dogs, too, on some of our many walks. Most people are surprised at seeing little horses.

Suddenly, Edward froze, then pulled backwards on the lead rope. "Rootbeer, look at that … that … that … whatever. Is it a dog? Aren't you a little afraid? It's as big as you are!"

"No," I said. "Look at his tail. He's wagging it so hard his whole back end swings back and forth, so he seems friendly. Only thing I'd watch out for is that drool coming out of his mouth. I don't want that on me. If we touch noses our whole faces will get soaked!"

We got closer—gradually, like always—and Lilly said, "How nice to see you again. Now our boys get to meet. This is Rootbeer and Edward. What's your dog's name?"

"This is Fred, a full-blooded Saint Bernard," the lady said. "He's very sweet, and I think he's taken a shine to your frothy-colored one, but both of your boys are very handsome."

The compliment made us stand proudly. We don't speak dog, but Fred's body language, his tail wagging and soft sniffing, were happy signs. They mean friendly in a language everyone seems to know, so we decided we could touch noses with Fred, the Saint Bernard.

Lilly told her friend that Fred was kind and handsome just like us and that she hoped we'd meet again.

As we walked away, Edward said, "What's full-blooded, Rootbeer? I mean, we're full of blood, too. I lost blood when I was sick, and the doctor had to give me more, so I know I'm full of blood."

"Maybe it's a term for special dogs. There are many things we don't know. We have to keep asking and learning," I answered. "Anyway, I like Fred. When we see him again, maybe we'll get to play together. Lucky for us he didn't get any of his drool on us."

We continued on, greeting walkers, joggers, and bicyclists. In between short chats, Lilly said, "Your manners are excellent, you are super fun to be around, and well, you are great horses." All that praise made us prance like parade horses.

Coming back near our corral, Lilly stopped, scratched our ears, and gave us special carrot treats.

"You two are doing so great, I think you're ready to have a job. Would you like that?"

Edward leaned in and whispered, "What's a job?"

Before I could think of an answer, Lilly continued. "There is important work you could do, and I believe you're ready for it. Having valuable work can add more to your lives, enriching you and others you meet. Playing and being happy here at the ranch is wonderful and also important, but a job that contributes to the lives of others would be a bonus."

"A job? Work? Enrich? Contribute? Lilly uses some strange words. What do they mean?" Edward asked me.

Lilly seemed even happier than her usual happy self. She hummed as she used the hoof pick to get out anything stuck in our hooves that could make us sore or even lame.

After cleaning our hooves, Lilly brushed our coats and reminded us what people do when they see us. "You cause everyone to smile. Remember all the smiles on our walk today? Even Fred, the Saint Bernard, was happy to see you."

Then she made the oddest statement: "You have an important purpose in life, and that is making people smile. You certainly make me smile every day. I'll explain further as I learn more details, but first I wanted to share the idea of working with you."

With that, she took us back to our corral, removed our halters, and slipped the long steel rod inside the post that keeps our corral divider in place.

"Thanks for the walk, fellows. I'm off to talk with the people in charge of a terrific program I hope we can join." With scratches on our withers but no more carrots, she smiled, waved good-bye, and walked toward her truck.

The second she disappeared, Edward hit me with a waterfall of unanswerable questions.

"A job? Work? Rootbeer, I don't know what she means with those words, but Lilly's right. Wherever we are, everyone smiles and says 'Hi.' Even people who start out with sad or frowny faces end up smiling when they see us, but that doesn't feel like work. Making people smile feels good, and it's easy. It is all natural, so how can that be a job?

"Are we going to do something?" Edward said, continuing his torrent of words. "What if I don't know how? Or if you don't know how? What will we do?"

"Whoooooaaa there, little brother. Slow down. I can't answer any of your questions, so I'll try to use logical thinking. Lilly used the words job, work, smile, important, and purpose all together, so maybe causing smiles can be a job. You're right about our walk today. People smiled, and that makes us feel good. I enjoyed it and you did too, right?"

He bobbed his head up and down in agreement.

"One thing I do know, Edward, is that all of our new experiences and changes have turned out well. Even your trip to the hospital had a good outcome. I must admit, even the Mini Play Day, when I got in trouble, turned out okay because of what I learned. We'll have to wait and see, but I think this will be all right, too."

Edward wasn't convinced. "We hear people complain that work is hard and tiring. They say they come to see their horses to forget work. Making people smile isn't either hard or tiring, is it?"

"I don't think so. Maybe there's more to doing this job, or perhaps work is hard sometimes but not always. Or work can be hard and fun too. Lilly went to a meeting and she seems to think we understand what she says—which we do. She'll tell us soon."

The very next day, Lilly came to the ranch in her truck, towing the mini-sized horse trailer she had used to take Edward to the hospital.

She jumped out and came in our corral to halter us, laughing and chatting away. "Well, fellows, are you ready to take a trip? It's time for me to show you that I finally learned how to drive this truck and trailer. If I can learn something as hard as hooking up, pulling, and backing up a trailer, you can do the job I have in mind

for you. You've already proven you learn quickly and conquer your fears."

Lilly's scratches were so soothing, we almost missed what she had said. Wait, trailer-pulling wasn't a new job for Lilly, was it? She took Edward to the hospital and both of us to Mini Play Day, so this wasn't her first time. We were confused.

"Part of learning about the trailer was easy, but wow, part of it was super hard," Lilly said. "First, I had to learn to back the truck straight, so I could hook the trailer up to it, so it couldn't possibly come loose. Then came the really hard part: backing up the whole thing and getting the trailer to go in the direction I wanted so I could park it, even in little parking places. Goodness gracious!

"When Edward got sick, I *had* to drive the trailer, so

I did. I was so worried about him I just had to be brave and do it, even though I hadn't practiced very much. All I wanted was to get him to the hospital. Once you were safely with the doctor, Edward, I knew I would figure out how to get the trailer out of there."

"Wow, Edward," I said, "I'm glad I didn't know that was Lilly's first time trailering. I would have been triple worried about you being sick and going to the hospital. Maybe I don't want to know everything."

"I was so sick I wouldn't have cared. But, Rootbeer, there's probably more to this story."

There was. "Fortunately," Lilly continued, "the hospital had a pull-through driveway, so I didn't have to back up. I knew there was a pull-through lane at the Mini Play Day park too. But I didn't want to be unprepared again, so I found a big empty parking lot where I practiced and practiced for six months. Thanks to my friend Tony, a patient teacher and coach, I learned how to do my trailering job.

"You fellows would have laughed at me because some of it was ridiculously funny, especially when the trailer went in the opposite direction of where I wanted it to go. I was so happy that Tony was the only person watching me learn.

"So now I'm confident about taking you fellows on our little excursion. Tony is coming with us."

"What's an excursion, Edward?" I asked. "Does it sound scary?"

"Ha! You are too funny, Rootbeer. Now you're asking me about a big word. Lilly got me to the hospital and home, and she said she's practiced a bunch since then. So, no, I'm not even a tiny bit scared to get in the trailer again. I don't know what an excursion is, but going anywhere is better than going to the hospital."

"Well, I'm sure you're right. I guess work can be both hard and fun if you have Lilly's attitude and keep practicing like she did," I said. "She kept trying, got better and more confident, and now she can laugh about it. If not, we wouldn't be going wherever it is we're going."

Tony arrived at the ranch as Lilly led us to the open doors at the back of the trailer. Pretending to be brave, I hopped in, followed by cool, calm Edward.

"You two are amazing! Katie did a great job teaching you how to get in the trailer."

Hmmm, there was that job word again.

"Little does she know how much practice it took for us to willingly get in and out of the trailer," Edward said. "Just like Lilly, we had to practice and practice, and now we can do it with no problem. It was hard in the beginning, but it's easy now."

Lilly praised us and gave us little carrots. She could see we are pros at trailering but we enjoyed the attention. Before closing the trailer door, she gave us her biggest happy smile. Making people smile seems pretty simple, so how hard can this job thing be?

"Too bad we don't get carrots for every smile," Edward said.

The truck engine started, and my thoughts quickly turned from carrots to wondering where we were going.

Hired

"That was quick. I didn't expect such a short ride," I said to Edward as we felt the trailer slowing to a stop.

"Me either," he agreed. "The hay bag Tony hung up was great, but I only got four bites before Lilly pulled into this large parking lot and stopped."

"We're here, gentlemen," Lilly called to us. "Wasn't that a great ride? I need to go find the program manager to see if she's ready for us. Tony will be with you, so keep eating, and I'll be back."

"Oh, good, more time to eat," Edward said, turning back to the hay bag. I was more interested in figuring out what was happening next than eating. The trailer is made of strong steel and has openings so air flows through, keeping us cool and letting us see out. I loved the smell and feel of the fresh air and looked forward to exploring the outside. Through the openings, I saw buildings, trees, and fences around the dirt area where our trailer was parked.

"Robin is ready for us," Lilly said to Tony. "She's very excited to meet you two minis."

"I'll get in the trailer and halter them, Tony. Let's keep the trailer door closed until both are ready to come out. Then I'll hand you Rootbeer's lead rope. Please open the door, giving him space, and ask him to come out of the trailer while I stay inside with Edward."

In my excitement, I surprised Tony by jumping out.

Tony looked at Lilly with a grin.

"I should have warned you that he comes out quickly. He loves to see what's around him. Give him a few ear scratches and he'll calm down while he scopes out his surroundings."

I was slightly anxious, but the scratches and remembering Mini Play Day reminded me to take deep calming breaths.

Once I was out of the trailer, Edward wanted out too.

Because Edward is littler than I am, the ground seems farther down to him. With Lilly holding his rope, he hung one front foot down, waved it around until he could almost touch the ground, and then he hopped out. I think it's cute how wiggly, excitable Edward is so careful. He stood looking around like I did, but in his case, he probably was searching for grass to nibble.

"This is all interesting, Edward, but I think you only want grass," I teased.

"Well, we didn't get to eat much on the way here," he said.

"You'll be fine, little brother."

Lilly, sensing my tension, said to Tony, "Rootbeer is a little unnerved, so let's switch around. Please take Edward, and I'll take Rootbeer."

They switched lead ropes, Lilly thanked Tony, and she turned to face the two of us, head on.

"Uh oh," Edward muttered. "Here comes the lecture."

"Before we walk anywhere, let's have a little chat, gentlemen," Lilly said. "Robin is the boss of the program we hope to work for, so we must make a good impression on her."

She looked back and forth between us and said, softly and gently, "You will be amazing because you are amazing. Let's go meet and greet."

"That wasn't a lecture," Edward said. "It was a pep talk!"

"We have to be very good and use our best manners. We can't get pushy at all, and we have to make Robin smile," I reminded Edward.

"I know. I am calm. You are the nervous one," he said. "Relax, we'll make Robin smile. We always make people smile."

Robin walked up to us with a big grin.

"See how easy this is?" Edward said. "We've got this work thing under control."

After greeting Tony with a handshake, Robin leaned down to us and said, "Hello, gentlemen. We're thrilled you're here."

"Robin calls us gentlemen, like Lilly does," Edward said. "It sounds positive and respectful, and it makes me feel grown up. I like her already."

I bobbed my head up and down in agreement.

"Welcome to the Helen Woodward Animal Center and the PET program," Robin said. "PET stands for Pet Encounter Therapy. I'm the lucky person that manages the program.

"Let's take a tour so you can see our center. We call it the 'Center' for short instead of using all four words." Whispering as if she was telling us a secret, she said, "Everyone is dying to meet you!"

Tony led Edward, and Lilly walked with me as we followed Robin. She guided us around the grounds, pointing out each building and its purpose and also what the various fenced areas are used for. Then we walked to a barn.

Edward's eyes were wide with wonder. "Look at all the other animals, Rootbeer. There are all sizes of dogs, horses, ponies, rabbits, snakes, and, and, and—what are those?"

We both stopped.

I looked up at Lilly, then at Tony, and then at Robin, hoping one of them would tell us what these critters were.

Finally, Robin said, "Have you gentlemen ever seen an alpaca before?"

I guess it was obvious that it was our first time, since we just stood there, staring. We still didn't get what it was, but it had a name: alpaca.

"Pretty cool, don't you think?" I asked Edward.

"Alpacas look like big furry pillows on long legs," he said.

"Great description, Edward. I love those super-long necks with fuzzy faces on top. Look at their beautiful eyes. They have the longest, thickest eyelashes I've ever seen."

"It looks like their heads could swivel all the way around," Edward said. "Now that would be very strange. Ha! I think it's funny that we're staring at them, and they're staring back at us. This is a first for us, and I'll bet it is a first for them."

As they were being led away, the alpacas continued to turn their heads, looking at us until they went around a corner and were out of sight. Maybe their heads do swivel all the way around.

"Think we can touch noses someday?" Edward asked.

"I hope so. I like seeing those alpacas."

"That was a great unplanned encounter," Robin said. "Let's continue our tour. So far, the little men are handling everything well."

While Robin led, Lilly and Tony walked us through several gates, up a slanted walkway, through little wooden buildings in a kids' playground, and then over all kinds of walking surfaces: dirt, grass, gravel, and concrete.

The funny thing is, Edward walked politely along Tony's side, looking everywhere and at everything. But me? My anxiety got the best of me again and I tried to run ahead. I felt an immediate tug on my halter. Oops!

Sternly, but gently, Lilly said, "Rootbeer, your manners, please."

Before Edward had the chance to tease me, I said to him, "I know. I can't believe I forgot again. I've got to do something about getting too worked up."

"Just breathe and trust Lilly," Edward told me.

As we passed by each building, people came out to see us. And, of course, they smiled. We felt like celebrities.

Robin put up a hand. "You can pet the horses and take pictures with them, but please, just a couple at a time. We don't want to overwhelm them. As you come up, please be sure they see you, and stand at their shoulders so you can reach their necks. Let them smell your hand, but as soft and lovely as their noses are, it's best to pet their necks."

"Robin knows a lot about horses and keeping everyone safe," I said to Edward. "No wonder she's in charge of Pet Encounter Therapy."

As we continued our tour, Edward turned to look at the biggest building.

"Hey, Rootbeer!" Edward said. "I know this place. It's the hospital I was treated in when I was so sick with colic."

The veterinarian and assistants must have heard the commotion outside, because they came running out. They crowded around Edward, all talking at once and telling him how happy they were to see him and how well he was doing. Edward loved the attention. It was so good to hear and see how much they liked my brother that I didn't mind being ignored.

"That man was my veterinarian," Edward said, nodding toward a man in a white shirt.

The doctor walked up and said to Lilly, in a voice loud enough for everyone to hear, "Edward was a perfect patient. He took his medicine without a fuss, and despite feeling lousy, he was gentle and kind to everyone who helped. We enjoyed having him here and were thrilled when he pulled through."

Then the doctor added, "Edward has great manners."

Was Lilly ever proud!

I don't mind telling you that I was learning a lot about my brother, and I was learning from him, too.

"That was just the icing on the cake!" Robin said, smiling at us and Lilly. "You minis passed all the tests with flying colors. Lilly, I hope you'll say yes to joining our family of volunteers. I think these gentlemen will be great ambassadors for the PET program everywhere they go."

"Well, gentlemen, what do you think?" Lilly asked. "It looks like you're hired."

We both bobbed our heads up and down, making everyone smile and laugh.

"I think that was a big 'yes!' from these fellows," Lilly said to Robin. "Gentlemen, Tony has some carrot treats for you to celebrate the great news."

Turning to Robin, Lilly said, "I've completed the general Center training and would like to schedule the PET special training as soon as possible, so all three of us are ready to start. What's next?"

We wanted to know too, so we stood and

listened carefully.

"Let's check the calendar to see what dates are good for you to take the training and then dates for the minis to go to visit a senior citizens' facility and a children's center. Once we set the dates, you and I will talk about guidelines, where to park, and how the horses will meet people." Then she added happy news for Lilly. "I'll do my best to find parking for your truck and trailer where you can pull through and around, like you did at the hospital."

In spite of how hard Lilly worked and practiced learning to back up the trailer, she was relieved at this news. Her preference is a straight-through parking place.

"Thank you, Robin," Lilly said. "We thoroughly enjoyed this visit. I am thrilled the minis passed the test. We'll be proud to be part of a great program like PET that's doing so much good for people and animals. Thank you for making the arrangements and inviting us to join you."

After goodbye hugs, and as we walked back to our trailer, I said to Edward, "I'm excited and agree with Lilly that being part of this program will be good. How about you?"

"Absolutely," he said. "I have a better idea about what our job is, and I'm not scared, but I still have lots of questions. Where will we go next? Will it be close to our ranch? Will the people be as nice as the ones here? Will Lilly bring a hay bag for us? Do you think there will be alpacas around or maybe some other animals we've never seen?"

"I'm not sure, little brother. But don't you think that's enough thinking—and questions—for one day? Like you said, we have to wait and see and trust Lilly. If I stay calm and you aren't too wiggly, we'll be just fine."

"Okay, but I want to know one more thing," Edward said.

"Oh, my goodness, Edward. Now what?"

Edward ignored my annoyed tone. "I want to know how much hay is left in the trailer."

First Job

Surprisingly, our first "job" didn't require a trailer ride.

"Each job will be special, of course," Lilly told us. "But we have a unique opportunity right here at our ranch."

We were as happy as she was that our first job would be at our own place where we're comfortable.

Lilly sounded wistful as she told us the circumstances. "A lovely, sweet four-year old girl named Tori is coming here to fulfill her wish of petting a horse. She is very, very sick, even more than you were, Edward. You two and gigantic Nico will allow her to fulfill this most cherished wish."

"Gosh, that's really awful," Edward said. "We will make sure she gets her wish."

I nodded. "Listen please, Edward. Lilly is whispering and explaining why this is extra special."

"This may sound simple, but Tori can't move," Lilly continued softly. "She will be lying down all the time because she can't move her arms or legs. She has a tube that gives her water, another tube for food, and a third tube to help her breathe. It's critical that we don't disturb any of the equipment helping her live. We need to be extra gentle and quiet."

"Did you hear that, Edward?" I asked.

"Remember when I was sick not too long ago?" Edward responded. "I wanted everyone to be quiet and gentle. Being sick is awful, and I know just what to do. But you've been a little nervous lately. Will you be okay?"

"I'll be fine. I know how serious and important this job is. I wanted to be with you and help you in the hospital, but I couldn't. This is our chance to help a sick girl, so don't worry about me."

"The three of us will walk to the large open space near the bridge entrance," Lilly said. "There's enough room for you three horses and lots of other people."

"We'll need a big space if Nico is part of this," Edward said. "He's a giant! In fact, I could walk under him."

"I thought of that too," I said. "Wouldn't that be fun? Nico is so sweet he'd probably let us do that, but I doubt any of the humans would."

"Why do you think they have Tori meeting big Nico and us little guys?"

"Maybe petting a giant horse and then us minis would be extra special for Tori."

"I'm excited to meet her, Rootbeer. We won't do anything to scare her or anyone with her."

As we walked to the meeting area, giant, white Nico was easy to spot among the crowd of people. He stood proudly, as regal and handsome as ever.

I saw a glint of metal ahead and said to Edward, "See all the poles with tubes? Lilly wasn't exaggerating. I bet Tori is in the middle of them. She must be really sick."

"You're right," Edward said. "You didn't see me in the hospital, but I had tubes stuck into me, and there were bags of stuff on poles that dripped liquid into me."

He spotted Tori and said, "Oh look! Tori has beautiful

black hair like I do. I wonder who all the others around her are."

As we approached, Lilly was introduced to Tori's mom, dad, sister, relatives, and friends who had come to be with Tori and see her wish come true. Then Lilly, Tori's parents, and Nico's person discussed the best approach for Tori. Nico's person suggested that Tori pet his big horse first and then pet us "little guys" next. Tori's parents agreed with that plan.

"I'm glad Nico is going first, Edward. We can watch carefully and learn what to do."

That's just what we did. We looked at this sweet girl and understood why everyone talked about how lovely she was.

"She's like a princess dressed in a lacy white dress, with long black hair, and long, long eyelashes—longer than the alpacas," Edward said in a soft voice. "All those tubes remind me too much of the hospital. I hope her doctors help her get well like mine did."

"Me too, little brother," I said. "It's scary that Tori needs those tubes to live."

"Yes, but Rootbeer, all the tubes and dripping stuff

made me better, so maybe these will do the same for her."

Tori's mom and dad said they could unhook her tubes long enough to lift her up to reach Nico's neck. Like us, Nico knew Tori was very ill, and even though his person held his halter and lead rope, he stood absolutely still. Tori's mom held her up and raised her arm, rubbing it on Nico's neck.

"Listen to everyone praising Nico. Now we know exactly what to do when it's our turn," Edward whispered.

When Tori's parents put her back down, they hooked up all the tubes again and turned her head toward us.

"Gentlemen, please take a little step forward so Tori can see you," Lilly said. We did as she asked. "Good. Now take one more step."

When we were about two feet from Tori, she said, "Let's stop here for now."

Lilly asked Tori's sister, who was only one year older, "Would you like to hold one of the mini's lead ropes?"

There was an outstretched hand and a huge smile. Her eyes shined happily as Lilly handed her Edward's lead rope.

"That was a good idea," Edward said. "I think she

was feeling left out because Tori gets all the attention. Tori is sick, but her sister is also a little girl, and she wants to be part of this, too. Don't worry, Rootbeer. I'll be as still as Nico was and make it fun for her sister."

"Edward," I said, "Lilly asked us to stop, but if you stay where you are, I think I can get closer to Tori. I think she'd like it. I want to show her how much we like her and want her to get better."

I took a half step forward and paused. When no one stopped me, I took another little step, then another, and then I was right near Tori's head. I stood there quietly, and when no one said anything, I reached out very carefully and put the softest part of my nose on Tori's forehead. I left it there without moving and stayed like that for a while. No one, not a horse or a person, moved.

It was a kiss from Edward and me.

When I stepped back, Edward nickered softly. "That was just right. See, everyone is smiling, especially Tori's mom and dad. But look, they're doing that weird happy-sad thing that people do. They smile and wipe tears from their eyes at the same time."

Just then, Tori's sister leaned down and kissed Edward on his nose. "I got a kiss too," he beamed.

"I am so proud of you two!" Lilly kissed and scratched us both.

As they got ready to go home, Tori's mom and dad thanked Lilly and Nico's person over and over again, saying how happy we'd made Tori, her friends, and her family.

"Your horses made her wish come true," her mom said. "Tori got to be with not only one, but three horses!"

Edward nudged me, "Since Tori can't move, how

does her mom know she's happy?"

As if she'd read our minds, Tori's mom said to Lilly, "Tori can still move her eyes and eyelids. She opens and closes her eyes to let us know how she feels. When she blinks fast, she's happy. She was blinking like crazy, so she is totally delighted!"

That made people do their happy–sad, smile–cry thing all over again.

Tori's sister came back over to Edward, stroked his back, rubbed his ears, and told him how much she loved him. The whole family came to pet us and thank us.

"Edward, Rootbeer, and Nico are the best horses in the whole world," Tori's sister announced to everyone. "They are the smartest and most handsome, too!"

"It was nice that everyone thanked and appreciated us, wasn't it?" Edward said. "And, I liked what Tori's sister said at the end, making everyone smile. Besides, what she said is true—we are smart, and handsome too if I do say so myself.

"You know the best part? Tori has her own special way to show she is happy. I'll bet Nico feels the same as we do. Big and little horses making a little girl happy—

how cool is that?"

Answering his own question, Edward said, "All of it was cool. I think your kiss made Tori the happiest."

After everyone hugged and said goodbye, Lilly couldn't stop talking as she walked us back to our corral.

"You were so careful with Tori, Rootbeer. That kiss you gave her on her forehead was the best gift ever. I don't know how you knew to do that, but you did. It was a magical moment. I could not be prouder of you two and Nico." Lilly paused, taking a white tissue from her pocket and dabbing her eyes.

"The three of you knew just what to do and granted Tori her wish. You were kind to everyone there. Edward, Tori's sister loved holding your lead rope. It made the day special for her too."

In the corral, Lilly removed our halters. "You seem to understand exactly what people need. There's no question that you'll do excellent work everywhere you go."

She scratched our favorite spots and gave us more carrots than ever. Helping such a sweet little girl was not hard work and felt important. We were so happy we really didn't need carrot treats, but we ate them just the same.

Edward was quiet all afternoon, and I took a long nap.

That evening, Lilly came to the barn carrying a chair. First, she led Kiefer to one corral and then put us in another corral next to him. She sat on the chair between our corrals looking at the three of us.

"What's she doing, Rootbeer?"

"I'm not sure. Thinking? Oh dear, are those tears in her eyes?" I asked.

Edward stopped nipping at my neck and looked at Lilly. "Oh no!" he said.

"I need to tell you guys something," Lilly said.

We held our breath.

"I thought doing the work of bringing smiles would be good for you and the people we see. But you know what? It touches me too. We're connecting to other beings and to each other. This is more than just fun. It's important. You touch my heart, and you'll touch others' hearts the same way. I feel so fortunate to have you in my life. Thank you."

After that, she sat back in her chair. She was quiet and wrote in a book she'd brought with her, filling what looked like empty pages. Gradually, it got darker and darker.

Lilly looked up from her notebook and said, "I better take you and Kiefer back to your corrals for the night while we still have a little light. There are extra carrots waiting for you and your big brother Kiefer as my thank you for being so special and sharing your unique gifts with others and with me."

As we munched our hay and carrots, feeling content, Kiefer called over to us.

"I appreciate getting carrots for your good work. Thanks! I wonder where you'll go for your first away visit."

11

Preparing to Work

"Guess what, gentlemen?"

"Lilly sure is full of energy this morning," Edward said. "Something's up."

"Our first off-ranch job for the Center is a place for young children. They are going to love you! We'll drive on a freeway, which I'm sure you did with Katie. There's lots of work to get ready, but I'll go fix your special food before I explain," Lilly said.

The minute we were alone, Edward started in with his "Rootbeer, what about ..." questions. "What? You have to work to get ready to go to work? What's the deal? I thought we just went somewhere and got people to smile."

I rolled my eyes. "You always say, 'Rootbeer this' and 'Rootbeer that.' It seems like all you do is eat and ask questions. Did you ever think that maybe I have as many questions as you do?"

Shaking my head, I thought, seriously, it's tiring to always be the responsible one.

"What can all these preparations be?" Edward continued, as if I hadn't spoken. "We took a short ride to the Center to meet people and animals, and here we walked down the aisle to meet Tori. Don't we just hop in the trailer, go somewhere, and make people happy? What's this place like? What's a freeway? Why do we need helpers? Who are they?"

"Edward, didn't you hear me? I told you I'm not sure either. Can't we just wait and see? Lilly said it was new to her too. Maybe she doesn't have all the answers. Trust Lilly to tell us what she knows."

Edward heard my frustration and became quiet. I don't know why I was annoyed—maybe it was my own anxiety. "I'm sorry, Edward," I said. "I didn't mean to be harsh."

"That's okay, Rootbeer," he said, returning to his hay.

Lilly came back with our special food and said, "My

little friends, tomorrow is our day to visit the children.

"You know Janet, Shar, and Gloria. We all took classes at the Center to train for these visits. For each visit we make, one or two of them will help us get ready and go with us. Isn't that great? This time, Janet and Shar will come."

"I like that our first visit will be to see kids," I said to Edward. "Maybe they'll be like Ali, Kasey, Reese, and Brogan—the kids we know. They are young, little, fun, and smart. They're younger than we were when we became brothers."

Without lifting his head from the hay, Edward nickered his agreement.

"Yesterday, when Janet was here taking care of her horse Snickers, I heard her and Lilly talking. Lilly told Janet this is an opportunity to bring smiles to kids who don't live with their parents right now."

"Big deal," Edward said. "We haven't lived with our parents since we were young."

"I know, Edward, but people are different. Most horses leave their parents when they're young, but most of the time kids live with their families for many years. Some live with mom and dad—or one of them—or grandma or some other person until they're grown up. These kids we're visiting live at this place for a short time until they return to their families or go to another home where they might be adopted, like we were."

"So, this is an 'in-between' place?" asked Edward.

"Hmm," I responded. "That's a good name—the In-Between place. When we visit, let's be extra sweet, because remember how sad and scared we were when we left our moms and didn't know where we were going? These kids might be worried, like we were."

"That's true," Edward said. "I left my mom and lived in two other places before Katie adopted me. When we didn't know what was going on with Katie, we were scared again. Being in-between can be frightening.

"Even when we lived here in this corral, we were in between having Katie and Lilly. Now we have Lilly, Kiefer, other big horses, and helpers, so it turned out well. I'm sure it will for the kids too."

"Yes, but right now," I said, "they are probably worried like we were and might not think it will be okay."

Edward went back to eating, and I pretended to eat so he wouldn't know I was uneasy. Our visit with Tori had been great, but it was here where we live and are comfortable. In-Between will be new, and we'll get there on something called a freeway. If I was on a freeway with Katie I can't remember what it was like.

I didn't like that the kids we would be visiting might be worrying about the unknown. I hoped they would laugh and smile, even for a little while. This felt like pressure, and you know horses don't like pressure. If this is what work feels like, maybe I won't like it.

"Edward, let's picture Tori's happiness and her special way of smiling and do our best to get these kids to smile in their own special ways," I said, trying to push my worry away and build my confidence.

"Sure," he said, mumbling with a mouthful of hay.

Lilly came in carrying two pretty halters. "These gorgeous new halters are only for visits, not for daily wear. Do you like them?"

She laughed, watching our heads bob up and down. "I'll take that to mean yes.

"Today, I'll prepare you for the visit. The kids are special, and they have loving adults who teach them and take care of them. Many people, both grown-ups and kids, have never been around a horse before, and even fewer have seen a miniature horse, so they will be excited. In fact, Robin told me that everyone is thrilled that you are coming."

I felt the pressure build, so I breathed deeply, remembering the pact Edward and I had made. I told myself we had done fine at the Center with people all around us, and with the crowd around Tori. We committed to helping each other be brave to give others a good experience, and that's exactly what we would do.

"So," Lilly went on, "to be sure it's a great visit, tomorrow morning before Shar and Janet arrive, here's what we are going to do. You will play in a big corral while I fix your special food and collect your gear and the trailer supplies. After play time, you'll eat, and then Shar and Janet will groom you, so you sparkle!"

Sure enough, bright and early the next morning, I could hear Lilly's truck and trailer rattling through the ranch.

Edward almost panicked. "She isn't going to take us before we eat, is she?"

"No. Didn't you listen yesterday? Only you would worry about getting enough food, Edward." I told him,

"Lilly told us we'd play and eat. She wouldn't let us go hungry, and frankly, you could stand to lose a few more pounds."

"Okay, let's go play," Lilly said, before Edward could protest or pout. "Kiefer is already out waiting for you in the next corral. I'm going to fill your hay bag full of Timothy hay and hang it in the trailer for you. I'll also fill a jug with water, take a pouch of carrot pieces for extra rewards, and bring brushes for last-minute grooming. Then we'll bring your new halters."

When Edward heard "hay bag" and "carrot pieces," he relaxed and was his fun-loving self again. He is so darn funny—and predictable. I was most excited about wearing my fancy new halter.

Lilly led us to the corral, where Edward simply stood looking out.

"Edward, I think she wants us to run around and work out our extra energy before the visit," I said.

With that, Edward nipped my back leg and ran off before I could catch him. Often that's how we start playing. He usually starts it, and I chase him around and around. If he gets too sassy, I kick my back legs at him, but never to hurt him. Edward has great reactions and is skilled at estimating how annoying to be. He's especially good at being just far enough away that my kicks don't touch him.

"Okay, my little friends," Lilly said. "Janet and Shar are here to groom you while you have your grain. I'll bring the trailer around, so you can get in without getting dirty. You will arrive looking your best to greet our special new friends."

"I don't like to be interrupted while I eat," complained Edward. "Why can't they groom us afterwards?"

"Would you like it better if you couldn't eat because we didn't have enough time?" I asked. That ended his complaining.

Janet and Shar brushed and brushed, using various kinds of grooming tools and then vacuumed us.

"Here, Shar, use this cream," Janet said. "It gets tangles out of their manes and tails, making it easy to comb through without pulling their hair."

"I use a product like this on my hair after I wash it," Shar said with a laugh.

They rubbed in the cream and combed our hair easily

and without any pulling. Tangles are not as big a problem for me because my mane and tail are not long or thick, but Edward is another story. His mane and tail are twice as long and thick as mine. Even so, it's nice for both of us to have our hair combed through easily.

Janet and Shar stood back, proudly surveying their work.

"They look terrific," Janet said. "This Show Sheen spray will give their coats an added glow."

"I know the last part is getting dirt and rocks out of their hooves," said Shar.

"Right. Wait until you see how good Edward is at this job," Janet told her. "The minute you lean over and touch his leg, he lifts his foot for you to clean it. You won't have to touch the next leg because he knows what you want, and he'll lift it right up for you."

"Why don't they have horseshoes?" Shar asked.

"They are what's called 'barefoot.' Horses with strong feet who spend most of their time on dirt don't need shoes," Janet explained. "A lot of people think being barefoot is best for horses' health unless they spend a lot of time working on hard surfaces, like concrete."

"You know a lot about horses, Janet. It's fun to learn about them from you and Lilly."

"Horses are special to me, Shar. I love everything about them. Besides how beautiful they are, I love how they feel and smell, how they look at you and take in everything in their surroundings. They're very in tune with nature and they make me notice more than I would otherwise. They soothe me like the ocean must soothe surfers, or how a forest can comfort and inspire hikers."

"Wasn't that nice to hear, Edward?" I asked him. "I didn't know Janet loved horses so much."

"I like that Shar asks as many questions as I do," he said. "That's how I learn."

Lilly brought in our colorful halters and said, "Getting your everyday halters dirty is normal, but we'll keep these clean, so they sparkle like you do. No rolling in the dirt when you're wearing these."

We both groaned.

Edward's halter was turquoise everywhere except the noseband, which had a pattern made of turquoise, purple, and white. My halter was green with stripes of yellow and orange on the noseband.

"Pretty fancy, don't you think?" I asked Edward. "Our lead ropes match our halters."

He knew we looked handsome.

"Hey, my friends," Lilly said. "You get to wear dress-up fly masks too. I couldn't find bright colors, but these with black-and-white checks will look elegant on you. The fuzzy black edges will help them fit snugly yet be very comfortable. I hope you like them."

Shar looked puzzled. "The masks cover their eyes. Can they see?" she asked.

"Here, hold this up in front of your face to find out,"

Janet said, handing Shar a fly mask. "The mesh allows them to see and also protects their eyes from flies and other bugs, especially in the summer when flies are everywhere and could cause health problems. In the trailer, something could fly up from the road and hurt them. These prevent eye damage."

"They're like our sunglasses," Shar said as she watched Lilly fit our masks on us.

"My fly mask is comfortable," I said.

Edward nodded that his was, too. "Our sunglasses make us look like stars."

Lilly opened the back of our trailer and said, "Okay boys, time to go! Your hay bag awaits. You can ride, dine, and look around. You have a restaurant on wheels."

"Why is the hay bag hanging at our nose level?" Edward asked.

"Safety," I answered. "That way, we can eat without getting our feet stuck in it."

As they closed and locked the trailer doors behind us, I heard Lilly thanking Janet and Shar.

"It's comforting to have you two riding with me. It helps to have extra sets of eyes to watch out for people who don't drive carefully."

Before we knew what not driving carefully meant, Lilly started the truck engine. The trailer moved, taking the five of us to our new adventure!

Kids First

"*We're* about to remember or find out what a freeway is, Edward."

Once we left the quiet, winding, tree-lined roads leading from our ranch, we felt our trailer speed up. Loud noises came from everywhere.

"Were you on a freeway with Katie?" Edward asked.

"Yes, but I don't remember it being enormous or noisy like this one," I shouted.

Motorcycles, cars, and trucks of all sizes and colors whizzed past and around us. Rows of vehicles seemed lined up on roads going the same way we were, only faster. No trees or grass were anywhere in sight, and the smells—ick! We crinkled our noses at the stinky smells and watched in amazement at all the speeding vehicles weaving in and out of lanes. I never imagined such chaos.

"They drive like there's some huge emergency and they all have to get to it," I said to Edward. "Lilly said we'd be on a freeway, but I didn't picture this. I'm glad she drives slower and doesn't care how many cars pass us. Going faster and zipping between other cars and trucks like these crazy drivers do would scare me. It will be a relief to get wherever we're going."

"Maybe that's why we hear humans say work is stressful. Just getting there could get on your nerves," Edward said.

He returned to attacking the hay with his usual gusto, but the commotion took my appetite away.

When we drove up to the In-Between buildings, we heard Robin's voice. Lilly leaned out her driver's window and Robin introduced her to a teacher who opened a set of giant gates. The teacher pointed to a special spot to park the truck and trailer. After Lilly parked, the teacher locked the gates behind us.

While waiting to get out of the trailer, we heard lots of voices coming closer. Lilly warned us to expect excited people, but we weren't quite prepared for what happened. I don't think Lilly was, either.

Before people could swarm around us like a human freeway, Robin held up her hands and said, "It's important for our animal friends to feel safe, so although you're eager, I need to ask you to wait. After the minis come out of the trailer and have a chance to look around, we'll have you come up two at a time."

"These people must work here, and gosh, are they enthusiastic," Edward said.

"Lilly, her helpers, and Robin will slow them down," I said. "Let's concentrate on making people smile."

The second we were out of the trailer, everyone talked at once.

"Can we pet them? Can we take selfies?" Without waiting for an answer from Lilly or anyone, a man squatted down by us, holding his phone out at the end of his arm. Click, click, click. He and a couple of other people took picture after picture. Edward stood wide-eyed and still but giggled at their happiness.

"Where are the kids?" Edward asked. "I thought we were seeing kids."

"Maybe they are behind these big people where we can't see them," I replied.

When the people finished taking selfies, they backed away, laughing and saying they would send the pictures to their families. They chattered about how cute we were and how they could hardly wait to hear reactions to the photos from friends, sisters, husbands—well, maybe everyone they knew.

Next, we saw four dogs. Edward stared, but managed to say, "Are all those dogs visiting too? Do they work here, or are we supposed to make them smile too? Boy, this is a wild day!"

"That it is," I agreed. "I remember Lilly saying there would be other PET volunteers like Shar, Janet, and her. These people and dogs must be who she meant. I suppose their job must be to make smiles, too."

"Thanks. In all this commotion, I forgot," he said as he started walking along with Shar.

The dogs wagged their tails, sniffing and greeting dogs they seemed to know, maybe from prior visits.

"I don't think they know that light-colored dog," I said. "She must be new to the group. See how interested all the dogs are, wagging their tails and taking turns sniffing her? I don't think I would like it, but she doesn't seem to mind."

"I wish we could wag our tails to show we're happy, but that's a dog thing, not a horse thing," Edward mused.

"We keep meeting dogs in every color, size, and shape," I said. "I'm beginning to like dogs more and more. Do you think they like us?"

"Maybe," he said. "I'd like to touch noses, but I suppose Lilly will ask us to meet gradually."

Quite frankly, I was happy to take it little by little.

"All we've seen are big people and dogs, Rootbeer. We are here to see kids, so where are they?"

"Be patient, my brother."

In the visiting yard, Robin directed the dogs to one area and pointed us to another one that was close to what looked like really yummy grass. Edward started to walk toward it, but Lilly noticed and stopped him. "Fellows, that looks like delicious grass, but it isn't real. It's artificial: made from chemicals. Eating it will make you sick."

Not only was Edward disappointed, he was horrified. "There's such a thing as fake grass? That's simply awful! Who thought up such a terrible idea?"

We looked at it longingly, wanting to try it for ourselves to be sure it was fake, but then we spotted the kids.

"Look, Rootbeer—kids," Edward said. "They're different sizes, shapes, and colors, too. Someone said they are seven to twelve years old. Since we're older, we'll have to set a good example and be role models."

Two of the kids wanted to rush up to us, but Robin asked them to line up for a turn. When they did as she asked, Lilly told them the best way to approach horses. All watched intently; some seemed timid and stood back. Others acted afraid, but we could tell they wanted to come closer. They were quiet at first, and then the questions came fast and furious.

"What are their names? How old are they? Which one is older? Are they boys or girls? Are they brothers? Sisters? Do they get along? How much do they weigh? Are they full-grown? What do they eat? Where do they live? Can we ride them? Do they like coming here to meet us?"

"Listen to them, Edward. They are just like you, asking

a million questions."

"See?" he said, pleased with himself.

Lilly answered every question while Janet and Shar walked us around our assigned area, away from the artificial grass.

Two of the children told Lilly they were brother and sister. They said they knew all about horses because they had horses at home and asked if they could take us for a walk. Lilly agreed and let Shar and Janet know it was okay.

"Each of you can walk a horse along with either Janet or me," Shar said. "Walking together, we can make sure you and the horses are safe. Are you twins?" Both smiled and nodded yes.

Lilly watched them with interest as they walked us.

"I can tell you know a lot about horses," she said. "You know how to walk them, to pet them with firm scratches, and to keep them away from that fake grass. You even know to stay away from their back feet. Would you help me explain to the other children how to handle horses and answer their questions?"

"Oh yes," they said in unison.

Turning to the circle of kids, Lilly said, "These two

are experienced with horses. They will show you the best way to handle them, so you and the horses are safe. They'll explain and demonstrate how to walk them and pet them and answer any question you may have."

The twins answered lots of questions, impressing Lilly, Robin, and the people who work at In-Between.

"Thanks. You did a great job," Lilly said to the twins. Then she said to the whole group, "I want to add one bit of information that hasn't come up so far. Horses don't kick to be mean, but if they get nervous, they might kick out. Even though they're little, a kick from one can hurt. Please let a horse see you approach and come up along their neck, not straight on or from behind. We call this the safe zone."

"Okay, who wants to come up and walk a horse?" Janet asked.

Several hands shot up.

"Each of you will get to walk with a mini," Janet said. "For the first round, one of the twins and either Shar or I will walk with you. Being calm is important. Do you think you can do that?"

Heads bobbed up and down. Everyone smiled, even the nervous ones.

"Edward, I think the twins are proud to teach their friends," I said.

"Well, they certainly are smart and know a lot about horses," Edward agreed. "They're good teachers. I feel safe and like walking with them."

When it was almost time to go back to our ranch, Lilly asked the kids, "Would you like to see Rootbeer's tricks before we leave?"

"Yes, please!" they all cried out.

"Let's do the Spanish Walk first, Rootbeer." Lilly gave me a special signal, and I began my fancy walk, the one where I pick my front knees up extra high, one at a time, creating an elegant-looking prance. I wished Lilly would tell them why it's called the Spanish Walk, because I don't know. Maybe she doesn't either, but it didn't matter because everyone liked it.

"Now for the trick everyone loves best," she said.

On Lilly's signal, I reared up on my back legs, my front legs high in the air. Everyone clapped, cheered, and yelled, "Again!" So I did, rearing even higher and earning a carrot treat from Lilly. She sometimes gives me a carrot for doing a trick—but not always. This time, she did.

"Time for us to go," Lilly said. "Thanks to all of you for a great time. We'll see you again."

"Gosh, that went too fast," Edward said to me as we walked to the trailer. "Look back, Rootbeer."

We both turned our heads back to the In-Between visiting area and saw nothing but giant smiles and waving hands. Kids; people who work there; other volunteers with dogs; Robin, Shar, Janet, and Lilly—everyone was happy.

As we continued walking to the trailer, we listened to calls of "Thank you! Come back! We loved having you visit!"

The fun didn't stop there. Just before Lilly asked us to go into the trailer, we met the dogs. Little by little, we met each one up close and touched noses.

"Next time we come, all these dogs will be our friends too," Edward said.

I realized that I didn't feel any pressure during the visit, so I think working will be okay.

"I think we did our job, little brother. The kids are happy. The adults are, too. Lilly said the kids and adults will talk together about their new experiences. Pretty terrific, don't you think?"

"Absolutely! Everything was perfect, except, that is, for the artificial grass," he sighed.

13

More Kid Time

"Weren't the kids cool?" Edward asked me when we returned from In-Between.

"They were. Maybe the shy ones will be braver next time."

With hay hanging out of his mouth, Edward mumbled, "The dogs were neat, too. I wish we could wag our tails to show them we liked them."

"Me, too," I said. "We can only swish our tails to chase away flies or show we're upset—a totally different message. I think we'll have to be horses and let the dogs be the happy tail waggers."

Edward chewed a while, then said, "Maybe the adults

there will be calmer next time. They were super kind, and I liked being special, but I felt closed in with all the picture taking. Did you?"

"A little," I said. "The good part is it wasn't scary because they smiled, and no one had a mad or angry face. Besides, Lilly, Robin, and the other helpers always make sure we are safe. I think some had seen horses before, but not miniatures like us. One person said we were a novelty. Think that means first time?"

"That makes sense," Edward agreed. "I know they liked us because it's easy to tell how humans feel. Every morning, I know Lilly is happy to see us. I also know what her stern face and voice mean when I forget my manners."

"Ha, that's how she gets your attention," I teased him. "You would probably ignore her if she was smiling."

"When she reprimands me, she bends down, looks me in the eye, and uses her 'I mean business' tone. You don't know what I'm talking about, since you're 'the perfect one.' It's irritating."

I laughed. "You're funny, Edward. Did you forget the talking-to she gave me after I dragged her down in the dirt at Mini Play Day? And how I caused us to get time out in the trailer? I know 'the look' and the tone of voice, too. I prefer the happy look and when she tells us what gentlemen we are."

We ate a while and then I said, "Edward, you were so quiet after our visit that I wasn't sure what you thought."

"Just because I'm quiet or wiggly or eating doesn't mean I'm not thinking. We're brothers, so we'll always share, right?"

"Deal," I said. "You have opinions about everything, and I like hearing what you think. Let's promise to talk after each visit, no matter how tired we are."

One day while Lilly was cleaning Kiefer's corral, Shar stopped by to say hello.

"Hi. I'm glad you're here, because I was about to call you," Lilly said. "Can you go to the In-Between place with me tomorrow? Robin called with a last-minute request. Janet can go."

"I'd love to," Shar said. "I wonder how the kids will react this time."

"Robin told me these would be different kids from the ones we met last time. She reminded me that kids don't stay long at In-Between. It's been a month since our first visit, so many children are back in their homes or with other adults who will love them and take care of them."

"That's right," Shar said. "I remember now. But the adults should be the same. We'll see if they are less excitable," she added with a laugh. "What time should I come?"

"Eight o'clock will give us enough time to get these gentlemen spotless."

The next day, Janet, Shar, and Lilly did our usual pre-visit routine. They groomed us until they decided we looked sufficiently handsome and led us to the trailer. Edward and I now knew what to expect on the crazy freeway, so we ate from our hay bag, ignoring the speedy drivers zipping around us.

"Oh, good," Lilly said when we arrived at In-Between. "There's a pull-through parking spot. I can back up pretty well now but pulling forward is less stressful."

I also said, "Oh, good," because the dogs jumping out of their cars were the same dogs as the ones from our first visit. Before going through the big gates, they wagged their tails, and we all touched noses.

"Edward, are you trying to wag your tail?" I asked.

"I thought I'd try, but it's still a horse swish, not a wag. Oh well, they know we're happy to see them."

"They do," I replied. "Our circle of different and unique friends is expanding."

Before I could say more, he said, "Here come the kids, Rootbeer. These are younger and smaller kids than last time. We can look them directly in the face." His black eyes glowed just like his black coat.

The staff stood back, holding hands with the kids and telling them about us. One adult said to Lilly, "We showed the kids those selfie pictures from last time so they would know what to expect and be prepared for the visit."

Pictures are great, but not the same as real life, and a couple of the kids seemed nervous but also curious about us. As Edward and I stood quietly, they became braver and asked to come closer.

Gazing around, Edward asked me, "What's that? That girl's chair has large wheels."

As I looked at the chair, I heard Lilly say, "That wonderful chair with wheels acts as the girl's legs so she can move around. It's called a wheelchair. Sometimes the big people push her, but she is learning to move it herself.

If she comes toward you, don't be afraid. Just stay calm and be your sweet, gentle selves." She scratched us and added, "You're such good fellows."

"Remember, Tori couldn't move at all," I said. "This wheelchair is magical. The girl can go where the walking kids can."

Lilly asked the girl if she could bring us closer. The girl nodded and when we got close, Lilly said, "Would you like to take one of the minis for a walk?"

The girl was so excited! She answered with a big smile, not words, and her arms and hands waved all over the place as if she couldn't control them.

"How will she walk us if she can't hold a lead rope?" Edward asked.

Lilly placed Edward's lead rope under the girl's hand on the arm of the wheelchair.

"Keep your hand here right here. Janet will help hold the rope, and your helper will push your chair, but you will be leading Edward."

Edward walked alongside the girl just like he does with Lilly and me on trails. They went all around the area. Somehow, Lilly knew the girl could do it. Our reward was a smile that made her eyes twinkle.

This was Edward's first time walking next to a wheelchair, and he knew it was special. He didn't wiggle or try to go to the artificial grass, and when they headed toward me, I saw that his eyes twinkled like the girl's. I could hardly wait to talk to him.

"Would you like to see Rootbeer's tricks?" Lilly asked. Of course, they did, so I took center stage. Since our first visit, Lilly had bought what she called a "magic wand," a two-foot-long sparkly stick with a star on one end. She uses it to signal me to do the Spanish Walk, or when she raises the magic wand, to rear.

All our practice paid off. Everyone clapped, cheered, and smiled at both tricks.

"Would you like to hold the magic wand and ask Rootbeer to rear?" Lilly asked the girl in the wheelchair.

She couldn't say the word, but from her wide grin, we knew her answer was "absolutely."

When Lilly put the wand in the girl's hand, she waved it all over the place. I knew she was doing her best, so as soon as the wand went up, I reared extra high. Everyone clapped and smiled, but the look on

the girl's face made me feel like I'd gotten a whole bag of carrots.

"Hey, Rootbeer," Edward said, nodding toward a tiny young boy who was walking on his tiptoes. An adult walked on each side, helping him. He made noises that didn't sound like real words. In some mysterious way, he let the adults know he wanted to pet us and lead us.

"Come on, Rootbeer," Shar said, leading me toward the boy. With his helpers on one side and Shar on the other sharing the lead rope with him, the boy and I circled our whole visiting area.

After another loop, Lilly asked the boy, "Do you want to try the magic wand?"

He nodded so much I was afraid his head would hurt. Lilly placed the wand in his hand and helped him make a fist around it. The second he raised the sparkly stick, I reared. Another success. My goodness, was he happy! The helpers were beaming, and I knew they would be happy all day, too.

"Edward, look how proud the boy is," I whispered. "I think walking me and getting me to do a special trick made him feel more confident, too. This is so much fun."

"We both had special kid moments today," he said to me. "I wish we had seen the kids from last time too, but I'm happy they're in homes where they're loved. I'm looking forward to our next visit already."

Not too many days later, Lilly told us we were going to make our third visit to In-Between.

"It will be another opportunity to make a difference, this time with ten-to-twelve-year-old kids," she said. "Gloria and Janet will join us."

When Lilly parked the rig (that's what she's now

calling the truck-trailer combination) she said, "Parking is getting to be a piece of cake." A piece of carrot sounded better to me, but oh well.

Everything was familiar—greeting the dogs, going through the big gates, and the reminder about artificial grass. Only the kids were new.

"Look at that, Rootbeer," Edward said, nodding to a boy who was dressed differently from everyone else. "I heard Lilly say he is wearing 'camouflage' like a soldier would wear. His boots are huge! He looks very serious. What do you think he'll be like?"

"We're about to find out," I said. "Here he comes."

Stopping a few feet away, the boy asked Lilly if he could walk up to us. Lilly nodded and asked Gloria to explain what we like and to give him some safety tips. Then Gloria asked the boy, "Would you like to walk Rootbeer?"

His shyness surprised us. He might have looked strong and serious, but he had a gentle manner.

"Why is his name Rootbeer?" he asked quietly.

Gloria smiled, rubbed her hand down my back, and pointed to my frothy hair. "The person who first adopted him thought he looked like a root beer float. Do you agree?"

With a slight smile, he nodded and cautiously reached for the lead rope. After walking me with Gloria, he walked Edward with Janet and then gave both of us good scratches.

"May I groom them?" he asked. His touch with the brushes and combs was firm and soothing.

"Thank you," he said to Gloria and Janet when he finished. "They are very nice horses." With that, the boy went to pet and walk the dogs. Before returning to his schoolroom, he came back over, patted us goodbye, and thanked Lilly for bringing us to visit.

Once he was back inside the building, an In-Between teacher came up to Lilly.

"That was wonderful. We almost didn't let him come outside because he has difficulty being with other kids. Sometimes he acts like a bully. He treated the horses and dogs with kindness and respect and showed us a whole other side to him. We'll use what we saw today to help him learn to be the same gentle person with people as he is with animals."

"That's surprising," I said to Edward. "People and animals are not always what they seem at first."

"He proved that," Edward agreed. "I believe horses and other animals know more about people than people often know about each other."

Lilly walked to her truck and came back with a hay bag. "Boys, since we'll be here longer than usual, here's some hay for you to eat during the rest of the visit."

While we ate, a girl who looked to be about twelve years old stood a few feet from us, leaning against a wall. She didn't talk or smile; she just looked down, like she was sad.

Janet stood by Edward and asked her, "Would you like to pet him?"

The girl didn't answer, move, or change her expression.

"That's fine," Janet said, smiling at the girl.

A few minutes later, Edward stopped eating, looked at the girl, and walked up to her, touching her hand with his nose. What? Edward leaving his food?

"I think he likes you," Janet said to her. The girl ignored Edward and Janet and kept leaning against the wall. She had a distant look on her face, as if she lived in a different world.

Edward walked back to the hay bag and ate some more. A few minutes later, he looked up, walked back over to the girl, and again touched her hand with his nose. Her eyes brightened. This time, when Janet asked if she'd like to pet Edward, her head nodded up and down a little bit. In no time at all, the girl was brushing Edward.

"Can we walk him together like the other kids did?" she asked so softly that Janet almost didn't hear her.

"Of course we can," Janet replied. "Edward would like that."

After the walk, Janet said, "Thank you for being so good to Edward. He enjoyed his time with you."

The girl looked into Janet's eyes and said, "Thanks for coming today." She looked at Edward and then back at Janet, giving each of them a tiny smile.

We nibbled our hay on the way home but were too tired to eat with much enthusiasm. Back in our corral and after having carrots and scratches from Janet, Gloria, and Lilly, I said, "Remember, we promised to talk about our day."

"Well, we never know what will happen on a visit," Edward said with a big yawn. "Each one is different."

"Today was special," I said, "but then each visit has been special. Still, I'm tired. Maybe this is what humans mean about work being tiring even when it's rewarding."

"Who would have thought kids have fears and challenges to overcome, like we do? Like learning how to be calm at Mini Play Days," he said with an impish expression.

"You'll never let me forget that day, will you, Edward?"

"Maybe ..." he said, then whispered, "... or maybe not."

Seniors Next

"*Youngest* to oldest!" Lilly told us.

"This visit, we'll meet older people. Many are grandfathers and grandmothers," Lilly explained as she cleaned our corral and filled our water buckets. "Janet, Shar, and Gloria—who you know and love—are grandmothers, so you'll like these people too."

"The word 'old' reminds me about Nico's person saying Nico is old and will retire soon," Edward said. "We're fourteen and fifteen. Is that old?"

"Wish I knew. Wait, Lilly is saying more."

"Gentlemen, the places we'll visit have names like

Senior Citizens Center, Assisted Living Residence, or Memory Care Home. The people are referred to as senior citizens, or just seniors, or residents. Some seniors can't move around like they did in their younger days, and some have difficulty remembering.

"I'm telling you a lot," Lilly went on, "but I like you to have an idea about what to expect. You'll be as big a hit with the seniors as you are with kids!"

Lilly walked over to halter Kiefer, and we started wondering and imagining what these senior places would be like.

"Since seniors have challenges, maybe they have helpers, like the kids at In-Between do."

"Gee, that makes sense," Edward agreed. Picking up on Lilly's enthusiasm, he was very chatty this morning.

"Maybe some get around in wheelchairs, like the cool girl at In-Between who walked us from her wheelchair. We're good being with people in those magical wheelchairs. I have a question, though."

"Of course, you do."

"What's wrong with questions?" Edward asked, acting hurt.

"Nothing, my dear brother. You are very curious and have an active mind, so you think up and ask questions. I shouldn't have teased you. I wish I had answers for your questions, but often I don't. I have questions, too, and questions help us learn. Anyway, what's your question?"

"Are memory issues like when I forget my manners and Lilly has to remind me?"

"That's one of those questions I don't have an answer for, but perhaps we'll find out on this trip," I said.

We knew it was visiting day when we heard the familiar rumble of our rig.

Lilly had us ready to go, so Shar and Gloria only had to do the last-minute shining up before leading us to the trailer.

"These handsome guys will thrill the residents," Gloria said. "I'm sure they've seen horses, and some had horses when they were younger."

"You're probably right," Shar agreed. "These guys may bring back special memories for seniors who had horses once. I wonder how many have met a miniature horse."

"Our helpers have questions too," I said to Edward. "We'll all be learning."

The minute we hopped into the trailer, Edward asked, "Where's the hay bag? Did Lilly have a memory issue?"

"Maybe it's a short trip, like the day we went to the Center and got hired," I told him. "Besides, we've been eating hay for an hour."

Off we went with Lilly driving very slowly through our ranch to the main road.

"Why does Lilly drive so slowly around the ranch?" Edward asked. "She only does that here, then we go fast on the roads and really fast on the freeways."

"I think it's some sort of rule. Lilly said something to Gloria about a three-mile-an-hour speed limit, so we don't startle horses or people. You know how Lilly is about safety."

"I do. Hey, we're slowing down already. You were right, Rootbeer. We just got in the trailer, and now we're here. Look at all those beautiful flowers!"

When Lilly saw the looks on our faces, she laughed and said, "The flowers are not for mini munching. Shar and Gloria will stay with you while I make sure we're in the right place."

"Rootbeer, this is nice," Edward said, looking all

around. "Besides the flowers, the building has big windows. I'll bet it's bright and cheerful, like our home."

We were waiting in the trailer when two women approached and said they worked there, helping the residents.

"We'd like to tell you a bit about our place and what we do," one of the women said. "Because some residents need help to move around, eat, get dressed, or take medicine, we have people who cook, serve food, wash dishes, and clean rooms. We also have gardeners, nurses, nurse assistants, and a doctor all helping our residents live happy, healthy lives."

"Edward, that's just what Lilly and others do for us." He nodded in agreement while continuing to stare at the flowers.

"Who is here to meet our residents?" the other woman asked.

"Two miniature horses, Rootbeer and Edward," Shar said.

The two women peered at us through the slats in the trailer. One exclaimed, "Oh my, those are two of the cutest animals I've ever seen! The residents will be delighted!"

"Time to meet the people!" Lilly said.

Our trailer is perfect for us, but for Lilly to halter us, she has to bend over to avoid bumping her head. She handed Edward's lead rope to Shar, suggesting that she walk him somewhere away from the flowers. I think he pouted. Gloria took my lead rope, and I hopped out too.

"Hey, Rootbeer," Edward said. "I expected one wheelchair but look at all of them! What are those silver things people are pushing? And the sticks they have?"

"I don't know what they're called," I said, "but we know some of the people can't get around well anymore because they have aches, pains, and special needs.

Maybe, like wheelchairs, those are walking helpers."

"I like all the moving-around helpers. Still, I wonder. Do you think not being able to get around easily makes them sad?" Edward asked.

"Maybe," I said. "But let's get the seniors to smile, like we do the kids. It will brighten their day and they'll forget about aches and pains for a little while." Edward nodded.

Suddenly everyone was talking, one on top of the other.

"They remind me of my horse when I was a kid."

"I've heard about miniature horses, but I never saw one before."

"I wanted a horse all my life, but I lived in the city, and I couldn't have one."

"Our family couldn't afford a horse."

"Do you think they're friendly?"

"They must be, or they wouldn't be here."

"Aren't they cute?"

"No, I think they're gorgeous!"

We saw lots of smiles and outstretched hands, but before we walked up to anyone, Gloria and Shar asked if it was okay for us to come closer. When people said yes, Shar walked Edward to one person, and Gloria took me to another.

Just like the kids, the seniors wanted to know all about us.

"I love that you want to know about miniature horses, and I love sharing information with you," Lilly said. "They're exactly like big horses, just smaller. Rootbeer is fourteen years old and thirty-four inches tall, measured right here on his back, a place called the withers. Edward is fifteen years old and thirty-one inches tall."

One man asked Lilly, "Will you be here long enough for me to get something from my room?"

"Of course," she answered.

Within minutes, he was back, holding a picture. "What do you think of this?"

"Fantastic!" Lilly said. "Look, fellows, isn't this wonderful?" She showed us the picture, then turned to the man and said, "I'll bet you were only a year old here. Imagine you sitting on that giant horse."

"Yes," he said proudly. "That was before my first birthday, and that's my grandfather's working horse. This great horse helped my grandfather plow fields and take crops to market. I'm eighty-seven years old now, but I remember that time clearly. I love my grandfather and this horse now as much as I did back then."

Other residents gathered around, looking at the picture taken long ago, and shared their own memories. People next to us scratched our necks and said how happy they were that we came. The man and his fellow residents talked and smiled, and then they talked and smiled some more. Everyone thanked us for coming.

"Thank you. It's our pleasure and we definitely will visit again," replied Lilly.

"This is your magic, gentlemen," Lilly whispered to us. "He remembered and shared this picture and his memories, and that helped other people think of happy times from their past. All this happened because you are here."

She hugged each of us and looked at us with tears in her eyes.

"There's that happy–sad thing again," I said to Edward. "I'm beginning to understand that it means something good."

We were about to leave when a bus drove in. The door opened, and a bunch of residents came out. They had been out doing some activity and were delighted we were still here.

While Shar and Gloria walked us closer to them, Lilly shared information like she had with the other residents.

"We have to leave soon, but would you like to see Rootbeer's tricks first?"

Again, like the kids, the seniors smiled and said, "Yes!"

After I did the Spanish Walk and reared (bringing the usual oohs and aahs), one lady asked, "What is Edward's trick?"

"His trick is being cute," Lilly said with a grin. The seniors laughed and laughed. I liked Edward getting attention, because I get smiles and carrots for doing tricks. Edward only gets smiles for being cute.

A nurse walked up to Shar and said, "I was feeling sad and glum when I came to work this morning, but now I'm happy and full of energy."

"That's wonderful," Shar replied. "The visits are for the residents and everyone who works here. Happy seniors and happy helpers make our visit a win-win."

A few sunrises and sunsets later, we visited another senior place called Assisted Living and Memory Care.

The day was super hot, but luckily, the drive was short.

The number of people waiting to see us surprised Lilly and Shar.

"I'll bet there are over forty residents here, plus all the helpers and family members, including some grandchildren," Shar said. "Fortunately, they have those two big white tents as sun shades."

"Shar," Lilly said, "with so many wheelchairs and people in regular chairs, let's split up. You and Edward can go into that tent, and Rootbeer and I will be in this one."

Some people wanted to touch us, while others only wanted to look. I walked around meeting people and did my rearing trick once.

When I looked for Edward, I saw him standing by a tiny, white-haired woman with a huge smile.

"Please bring Rootbeer over here to meet this woman," Shar called out to Lilly. "Tomorrow is her one hundredth birthday! Wait until you hear what she did on her ninety-ninth birthday."

"Last year, my aunt's wish for her ninety-ninth birthday was to ride a horse," the woman's niece said. "Guess what? She did it! That was at the Helen Woodward

Animal Center. The Center made her dream come true."

"Gosh, the Center does a lot of wonderful and cool stuff," I said to Edward.

On our drive home, Edward and I nibbled hay and talked about the people we'd met.

"Many people had horses when they were younger," I said. "One lady even had two minis. I wish she'd said their names. Who did you meet, Edward?"

"I also met people who said I reminded them of horses they once had. But I wondered about all the people who didn't smile or move, and I thought maybe those were ones without memories any more. One did reach out and touch me softly on the back, so maybe that was a memory. Their helpers smiled a lot, and we know that's good."

"Yes, I think we did our jobs well," I said. "On the way out, I met a man who, in a whisper, told Lilly he'd been a horse and cattle rancher for fifty years. Imagine that, Edward. He scratched my neck and said he was lucky to have such a great life."

"I'm glad we both got to meet the woman who rode a horse at ninety-nine. I'm not sure what ninety-nine is, but if I could be like her, I'd like to be ninety-nine."

Many days of playing and eating went by before Lilly took us on another adventure.

This trip was a long, long drive to a senior citizens center that had a lovely courtyard. We saw the residents waiting for us and immediately, one lady asked about a million questions.

"She asks more questions than you do, Edward."

"I think you're right," he agreed.

Many of her questions were the usual, like about weight, height, and age. Then she went on and on: "How long do miniature horses live? Do they wear horseshoes? If not, do their hooves get trimmed? How often? Do they see a dentist, and if so, how often? What tools does the dentist use? Does a veterinarian give them the same shots they give big horses?" After pausing and taking a deep breath, she said to Lilly, "Am I asking too many questions?"

"Of course not," Lilly said. "We love questions." We stood quietly and listened to Lilly's responses.

"They see a dentist once a year and any time I think either one has a problem. Horse dental health is as important as human dental health. Their veterinarian gives them disease prevention shots at the same time he gives them to my big horse, Kiefer. The farrier trims all their hooves on the same day too—every six weeks. Having all three on the same schedule is easiest.

"With good care, these two sweethearts will live long, healthy lives." People liked hearing that—so did we.

Lilly noticed a man sitting in a cool, shady area, looking at us and smiling. "May we come over?" she asked.

He nodded, and Lilly led us over to join him in the shade. Immediately, the two of them started talking about horses.

"I trained hundreds of horses over many years," he said. "I even trained a grand champion horse that won all kinds of titles at horse shows around the country and is in the Quarter Horse Hall of Fame. His name was Peppy San Badger."

"That's the father of my trainer's horse, Peppy!" Lilly exclaimed. "Her name is Debbie and I can hardly wait to tell her. She will be thrilled."

Another man walked over to Lilly. "You may not know, but these visits mean a lot to us," he said. "Thank you for coming, and please come back."

When it was time to leave, Gloria and Shar led us

to the trailer while the head of the senior center talked to Lilly.

"Absolutely everyone loved meeting the horses and reliving good times from their past," she said. "Thank you to Rootbeer and Edward, who made everyone's day better."

Edward jumped into the trailer ahead of me and then, with a mouthful of hay, said, "That was fun—I wonder where our next job will be."

Animal Second Chances

Soft evening shadows and the sound of frogs chirping and croaking in the creek put me in a mood to consider the life Edward and I shared.

"Edward, over the past few months, we've been many places and met many people. I wonder, what do you think about it all?"

"I love that question," he said. He thought a while before replying. "We've had experiences here and all over outside our corral that I could never have imagined. Did you know all that was out there?"

"Not at all," I agreed. "But what do you think about

it? Do you like working? Would you rather stay here enjoying our pleasant daily routine?"

"I like both," he said. "Why are you asking? Are you unhappy with playing and having a job?"

"Here's what I've been thinking, Edward. I loved our life with Katie, and then I was scared when she was leaving. Once Lilly started taking care of us, I learned to trust her like I trusted Katie. The routine of our life was peaceful and easy, and we knew what to expect. Then Lilly helped us improve our manners, and once we did that, everything was good again. But then we started working, and—"

"You don't like working?" he interrupted. "You seem to."

"I do," I said. "I think it makes life more interesting. We're learning, and we're better about facing new challenges. Making people smile feels good."

"Well, then," he said, "what has you worried?"

"Not too much, I guess, but we've had so many changes that I wonder about the future. Sometimes I think it would be good to only think about today, like we used to, and like other horses do."

"Can't we be excited about the future and enjoy our daily routine?" Edward asked. "We know Lilly prepares us for whatever is coming—that is, if she knows," he added. "There are always unknowns, like when I went to the hospital. Worrying doesn't help."

"You are pretty smart, Edward." I sighed and added, "I know I worry too much. Actually, I like making smiles and having new adventures together as brothers."

"Does that mean you like our new life?" he asked.

"I do," I answered. "But there's one thing I don't like."

"What?"

"Freeways!"

"I agree," Edward said. "The noise, the smells, the fast driving—I don't like any of it."

I laughed, and we resumed eating quietly. After a long silence, I said, "Thanks, Edward."

He nickered, continued eating, and mumbled something like, "No problem."

When Lilly arrived, she had an expression that told us something new was up. I glanced over at Edward who shook his mane, and for the first time ever, he gave me the look. We turned to Lilly to listen.

"Robin asked if we'd like to visit a new place—a special school for teenagers. They are about the same ages as you, fourteen to eighteen. Robin told me the students, principal, teachers, and staff are wonderful, and they're absolutely, positively dying to meet you. PET animals and volunteers have been going there twice a month for over two years." Hardly taking a breath, Lilly rushed on: "I didn't hesitate a second and told Robin we would love to go."

She kissed the tops of our heads and left to go to her tack room. Before she was ten paces away from our corral, Edward started in.

"What do you think is so special about this school, Rootbeer? Lilly believes that everywhere we go and all the people we meet are special, but she seems extra excited about this one. Do you think it will be like the In-Between place only with taller people and like senior centers but with younger people? If kids who are fourteen to eighteen are 'teenagers,' I guess that makes us teenagers."

"Good questions, and just what I was wondering, Edward."

"I figured out that wondering and questioning are like

putting together pieces of a puzzle, Rootbeer," he said. "It makes my mind work harder."

"Well then, having a job is giving our brains a lot of extra work."

"You can say that again!"

The next day, near our corral, Janet and Lilly chatted while saddling their horses, Snickers and Kiefer. When we figured out they were talking about the school we'd visit, Edward and I went to the front of our corral to listen.

"I used to teach at a school like this, and I loved it," Lilly said.

"What makes it different from the typical big high schools?" Janet asked.

"Students attend this school for various reasons," Lilly explained. "Some fell behind in their classes at another school, so they go there to get more individual attention, catch up on classes they missed, and graduate from high school. Other students don't like attending a big school and prefer a smaller school. Still others were kicked out of their schools and assigned to this school."

"Fascinating," Janet said. "It sounds like this school suits some students best."

"Yes, it does," Lilly agreed. "Schools like this make a world of difference in many students' lives and futures. Everyone knows everyone else; teachers have fewer students and can guide them closely. Almost all the students do well and achieve their goals."

Janet was quiet for a moment and then said, "I would call it a second-chance school."

"That's a perfect description, Janet."

Edward perked up, nickered softly, and said to me, "Hmm. Janet called it 'second-chance.' Maybe that's what we got too. After Katie, we have Lilly, like a second chance. I think that's what the In-Between place is too."

Edward's comment made me realize how much that little guy astounds me. I do give him grief, but he's not just cute, he's very wise.

A few days later, Lilly pulled up in the rig and off we went to the high school. Gloria and Shar went with us and we heard Lilly tell them that Janet would come on the next visit.

Bright orange cones marked our parking spot in front of the school. A man whose name tag said "Mr. Henry," came up and said, "I thought you'd like a special spot where you can pull straight ahead and out when the visit is over."

"Mr. Henry, you are my hero," Lilly said, laughing. "Not only do you keep the whole school tidy and running well, you've made this a perfect start to our visit here."

After Lilly haltered each of us, she handed Edward's lead rope to Shar and gave mine to Gloria. They each asked us to come out of the trailer and walked us around the parking lot for a few minutes. They know we like to see our surroundings when we are someplace new. Edward and I raised our heads high, took in the new smells, and looked at the surrounding greenery and the school inside a high wire fence.

When Robin arrived, she suggested that everyone meet first in the parking lot. "These dogs and minis don't know each other, and we have two other critters they haven't met: a snake and a bunny."

"Wow," I said to Edward. "More new and different friends. I wonder what the snake does? How do you pet one? Does the rabbit hop around? How many dogs do you think will come?"

Seeing Edward bobbing his head up and down, I

asked, "What's so funny?"

"Now who's asking all the questions?" Edward quipped.

"Hey! I have a question for you, Rootbeer. Look at that ball of fluff. Is that the rabbit?"

"Gentlemen, meet my dog Balonee," Robin said. "People love touching him because he is so soft and sweet. He looks like a puppy, but he was about eleven years old when I rescued him. He has a hard time walking for very long, so I take him to meet the kids in this baby stroller."

"That's like a wheelchair for dogs," I whispered to Edward.

"Wheelchairs, walkers, and canes help the seniors move around, and don't forget the little girl in the wheelchair," Edward said. "What will people think of next? They're all such great inventions. Can you imagine if Lilly took us around in some sort of wheel chair?" That made us both snort.

"Have we met the dogs coming today?" Shar asked.

"They are all new to the mini team," Robin said. "Cody is a rescue through the Center too, like Balonee. He's a mixture of breeds. Another dog, named Solo, is an Afghan Hound who joined his family from the Afghan Hound Rescue. The snake and the bunny are also rescues. They live at the Center, not in homes like Cody and Solo, so the staff at the Center is their loving family."

"Wonderful," Gloria said. "While we're waiting for everyone to get here, please tell us Balonee's story. We'd like to hear it."

"About a year ago, someone dropped him off in a parking lot inside a carrier with a note from his owners pinned to his crate," Robin said. "The note said they were very sad but couldn't take care of Balonee anymore and that they trusted that whoever found him would see that he got a good home. No one had signed the note. It said, 'THANK YOU!' in big letters.

"Fortunately, he was brought to the Center, where he could be fostered until he was healthy and ready to be adopted.

"I went to the people in charge of adoptions at the Center," Robin continued, "and told them I'd foster Balonee until they found the right home for him. Guess what? After a week, I knew that my home was the right home. So now Balonee is my partner and goes on PET visits. He's a huge hit with everyone. I adore him!"

"That sounds like us, going from one loving home to another," I said to Edward.

"Yes, it does," Edward said.

"Oh good, the other dogs are here," Robin said as a car pulled into the parking lot.

A minute later, Edward and I had a startling moment that left us speechless.

Fifty feet away, out of the back of a car came this huge animal with long, gray, silky, flowing hair. I whirled around to look at him with my eyes so wide open the whites showed.

When I finally found my voice, I whispered, "Edward, is that a dog?"

Edward neighed a big hello to whatever it was. "I think so. Doesn't he look cool? Don't be scared, Rootbeer. He's only my size."

"I'm not scared, just surprised," I said. "Do you think that's the one Robin said is the mixed breed dog or the Afghan Hound? He's quite beautiful...at least, I think it's a 'he.' I've never seen an animal with long hair like that. He's elegant and graceful."

Then I laughed.

"What's so funny, Rootbeer?" Edward asked.

"I just realized that I acted the same way that some big horses do when they first see us. Their bodies stiffen, their eyes get huge, and sometimes they back up. Once they figure out we're not a threat to them, they relax and become curious. My reaction helps me understand why the big horses act that way. This dog isn't any more a threat than we are."

Solo sat quietly by his person. Clearly, he was a dog, but different from any we'd seen.

Lilly leaned down, scratched behind our ears, and said, "That's Solo, the Afghan Hound. Isn't he gorgeous?"

We sensed that even though he sat quietly, he

wanted to play. We were all curious about each other, and gradually, we were allowed to step closer to him. Solo sat waiting and wagging his tail back and forth on the ground. Although I remained cautious, Edward was feeling Solo's happy spirit and wanted to play. Then we heard Shar ask Solo's person, Liane, to share his story.

Liane stroked Solo's neck and back as she talked. "He was about four years old when he ended up with the Afghan Hound Rescue. I don't know why or how he got there, but we've been together three years, and I'll tell you, meeting him was my lucky day. He is a joy every single minute."

Another woman got out of her car, followed by a little yellow dog that Robin called Cody. He wiggled all over like Edward always does and seemed excited to see us. While everyone chatted away, we heard Cody's person say, "People say we rescued these dogs through the Center. I think they rescued us, because they enrich our lives. I fell in love with Cody at first sight!"

"That's exactly what Katie said about each of us," Edward said to me.

"You're right, but just a second," I replied. "Lilly is

saying something about us." We like it when she talks about us.

"Well, I didn't find Rootbeer and Edward at the Center, but I'm just as grateful that I got to adopt them from their previous person, Katie. Aren't we all lucky?"

While all the humans nodded, we turned to Cody, who was tiny and had curly yellow hair and none of Solo's patience. Without hesitating, Cody managed to wag right up to us so we could meet nose-to-nose.

"Cody is super cute, even though his front feet turn out in an unusual way and his bottom jaw sticks out farther than his top jaw," I said to Edward.

"I know. I like it because it looks like he has a permanent smile. I'll bet he's happy all the time."

"Edward, Cody seems to think he's a big dog, like you think you're a big horse."

"Well, we are big, Rootbeer! We're big enough. Besides, it's all about how you feel inside."

"Both Gloria and I adopted two wonderful cats from the Center," Lilly told the other volunteers. "We're fortunate that the Center takes in dogs and cats. Center people make sure they are healthy, and they help them learn good manners and how to get along with others so they are ready to be adopted into 'forever homes.' Our community is so fortunate to have the Center and other second chance places."

"Lilly and I volunteer at a horse rescue organization that offers the same services as the Center, only for equines," Gloria added. "That rescue has even taken in a few donkeys."

"Gosh," said Edward. "Lots of people help animals get second chances."

"You're right, Edward. It makes me wonder if Lilly hadn't asked Katie to give us a second chance if we might have gone to the Center or a horse rescue place. Anyway, we and all the other animals are lucky. I'm happy the people who rescue or adopt us feel the same."

"I hope Robin will tell us about the snake's and bunny's second chances sometime," Edward said.

"Me too," I said, "but, that will have to wait because we're about ready to go through those gates and meet second-chance teenagers."

16

Teenage Second Chances

"Come on in," Mr. Henry called. "Everyone is waiting and happy to see the dogs, the bunny, and the snake again. And we're very excited to meet our two new guests, these miniature horses! Please follow me through the gates."

Gazing around, Edward observed, "Every place we visit has fences, locked gates, or locked doors on the buildings. It reminds me of the ranch with everyone here living in a huge corral. What do you think, Rootbeer?"

"Hmm, interesting idea, and another of your fascinating observations," I answered.

Before I could think of an answer, Edward added, "Katie had a fence around her house, and there's a fence around our ranch and the arenas."

"People corrals. Hmm, maybe you're right and people feel safe in corrals, like we do in ours," I said.

Gloria and Shar led us into the courtyard while Lilly met and shook hands with students and teachers. A man walked up to her with a big smile, and they hugged!

"How great to see you again, Chuck," she said. "I loved working with you all those years ago. Congratulations on running this terrific school."

"Thanks," he said. "We had a great time back then. I wish we were still working together."

"Gentlemen," she said, turning to us. "Meet Principal Chuck, the head of this school. He'll introduce you to everyone soon, but first, we need a few minutes to catch up."

"Lilly and Principal Chuck hugged," said Edward. "Do you think handshakes are for people who don't know each other but hugs are for when they know and like each other?"

"Once again, your perceptions, insights, and

conclusions amaze me, Edward."

"As do all the big words you come up with," he teased.

"Welcome, humans and animals," Principal Chuck announced to us and everyone in the courtyard. "Thanks for coming. We love the PET program, and we're thrilled to welcome back our returning friends and to meet two new ones, these handsome miniature horses. Thank you for expanding our school's PET family."

As Principal Chuck spoke we took in our surroundings. Sidewalks crisscrossed the courtyard with patches of grass in between. Classrooms surrounding the courtyard were painted light brown with bright blue doors.

"Look at the grass, Rootbeer. And smell it. This is the real deal, not that artificial junk!"

"Remember your manners, dear brother. Let's not get in trouble on our first visit," I cautioned him.

After meeting the faculty and staff, Lilly asked Robin, "What's the best way for students to meet the minis?"

"The dogs, the snake, and the bunny will meet students in the classrooms," Robin said. "The minis can be here in the courtyard. Teachers will bring their students out one class at a time."

"I like that idea, Robin," Lilly said. "I brought a hay bag along to keep them from eating your grass, Principal Chuck."

"Well, rats," Edward moaned. "Hay is better than nothing, but the grass looks and smells yummier. It makes my tummy rumble."

Almost on cue, I heard Edward's tummy rumble.

"Hear that, Rootbeer? Lilly says rumbly noises in our tummies are a good thing. It means our insides are working well and we're less likely to get colic. I sure don't want to go through that again."

"I certainly hope it doesn't happen again either," I said. "Here comes Lilly."

"Gloria and Shar, it's okay for the minis to eat from the hay bag until students want to walk them," Lilly said. "I'll answer the students' questions."

When the first class came out, I said to Edward, "They act just like the little kids, only they're taller. I see some who want to come right up and others who act afraid. We can't be that scary to them."

"That would be strange," he said, "since many of them are bigger than Lilly. Look at that girl standing next to the teacher. She acts like she wants to come closer but seems scared, or maybe a little nervous."

As he said that, her teacher wrapped her arms around the girl, and together, they walked toward us as if they were one person. I stood without moving until the girl gave me the smallest little tiny touch on my back before hurrying away.

"Look at her. She seems proud of herself, don't you think, Edward?"

"I do," he said. "She's standing over there smiling as if she's done something very brave. Maybe it was brave for her."

"May I hold a leash and walk one of them?" another student asked.

"Of course," Shar and Gloria answered in unison.

Soon another student asked, and then another.

"They look like a dog's leash, but we call these lead ropes," Shar told them. "Each of you will have a turn. Gloria or I will walk along and coach you, so you learn the best way to walk safely. Keeping you and the minis safe is vital and will ensure we all have a good time.

"When they walk next to you, put some slack in the

lead rope. They won't feel any pressure, which tells them they are walking just right. If they go ahead or fall back, give a gentle tug until they are back next to you again."

Student after student walked us, until I think we did a million laps around the courtyard. We definitely got our exercise for the day.

One really tall, lanky boy came up. His cap was pulled down so far on his head it almost covered his eyes, like he was shy or upset. He acted like he didn't want to walk with me.

"Are you afraid or are you just too cool to walk the horse?" one of his friends asked, giving him a little punch in the arm, kind of like Edward used to push with his head.

"I'm not afraid or too cool, dude." Turning to Gloria, he said, "May I have the lead rope?" He really was acting super cool—like it wasn't a big deal and he didn't care—but as we walked, he couldn't help smiling and giggling too. He was happier and friendlier than before our walk. People sure are unpredictable.

After all the classes had turns coming out, a bell rang, which signaled the start of student lunchtime. As they went to line up, several students asked if they could take "selfies" with us. We've gotten to be pros at people taking selfies. Since they are guaranteed smile-makers, we're happy to do them, especially with new friends.

As our time there ended, Principal Chuck walked with us to our trailer. "Thanks for coming," he said. "Everyone

loved this visit, and we're already looking forward to seeing you next month."

"I like this school," said Edward. "I'm glad we get to come again."

"I think most of the kids were around horses for the first time today, and seemed to enjoy it," I said. "I wonder what the scared girl and the cool guy will be like next time."

The next month, we arrived and parked in our same special orange-cone place. Lilly had told us earlier that a newspaper reporter was coming to learn about PET and write a story for his paper.

Robin, who always meets us at our visiting places,

introduced everyone to the reporter.

"All the animals will be in the story, but you gentlemen are the main attraction because you are the only minis in the PET program," she said.

"The title of your story can be Mane Attraction," Lilly said to the reporter.

That made him laugh, although we weren't quite sure why. Some people jokes don't make sense to us.

As Shar and Gloria took us to meet the students, Lilly walked with the reporter, answering his questions. We heard her say, "You must be good at your job because you ask great questions."

"You should be a reporter, Edward," I said, nudging him. "You'd be amazing."

"Thank you, Lilly," said the reporter. "I love my job. I research a topic, ask lots of questions, take pictures, and write a story. The PET volunteers and animals do wonderful work, and I'm happy to offer our readers the opportunity to learn about the program and this terrific school."

The reporter followed us around, asking students questions and taking pictures, even taking photos of the students taking selfies.

As the reporter finished up his notes and photographs, Lilly thanked him.

"We appreciate you doing this story," Lilly said to him. "I hope when people see the pictures and read about Rootbeer, Edward, and the other animals, they'll understand how important programs like PET are. People know that humans help animals, but animals benefit people, too. You probably know, but there are scientific studies showing how animals reduce anxiety in people and lower their blood pressure. I call that the best kind of medicine."

"I couldn't agree more," he replied, nodding and smiling.

Back in the parking lot at the end of the visit, Principal Chuck gathered everyone together for a picture of the volunteers, the animals, and Mr. Henry. The snake and the bunny couldn't come out, so only their travel boxes were in the picture. Getting a bunch of people and animals to hold still and face a camera isn't easy, but we managed.

Principal Chuck asked the reporter for copies of his pictures, saying, "With your photos, along with the ones the students and teachers took, I'll make a PET wall. One entire front office wall will be student and PET photos, which will be a big hit with the students and their families. To be sure you know, we got permission from parents to take and use these photos."

After the final goodbyes (people seem to like long goodbyes), Lilly and Solo's person, Liane, talked in the parking lot. They looked over at us and saw Solo touching noses with Edward and me.

"That looks like a high-level meeting about serious matters," Liane observed.

Each of our first two visits to this special school were different, but the third one—wow, what a to-do!

While she was getting us ready, Lilly warned us that the media would be there. "That means not just one reporter but lots of them, and television people, too."

"We know what a reporter is, but what's a television? And what does media mean?" Edward asked.

"I don't know what television people are or look like either. It's another of our adventures with Lilly, and one of those mysteries that will be solved when we get to the school," I said.

As we pulled into our bright-orange-coned parking spot, we looked out from our trailer and saw lots of people with notepads, cameras, video cameras, and microphones.

"That's the media, gentlemen," Lilly said as we came out of the trailer. "They're all here to see you and the other animals. They have equipment to take pictures and videos, and to ask questions."

"Well, that answers our questions about media, Edward. They look like all the other people only with equipment."

We expected a ton of questions because of our experience with the reporter last time, and we knew about cameras, but we didn't know about huge video cameras. One cameraman followed us on walks and said, "You guys are going to be on TV. What do you think of that? You might become famous."

"How do they put us on or in a TV, whatever that is? Aren't we already famous?" Edward mumbled to me. "Isn't that why they are all here? Besides, what does famous mean?"

As students walked us around with either Janet or Gloria, the media people asked question after question, writing the answers on page after page of their notebooks. They took tons of pictures and videos of us with the teenagers. We listened closely when they asked one teen what she thought of us.

"I love when the animals visit. We learn about each of them, and maybe they are learning about us, too. All of them are kind to us, and very gentle. They make us smile and feel happier after they've been here." Other kids echoed these sentiments, and one added, "They are nicer than lots of people." Many of the teens agreed with that.

"Well," I said to Edward. "Smiles and happiness are our job. I'm glad they say we do it well."

One media person put his video camera down low, close to the ground, to get pictures from our eye level. Being curious, Edward and I put our noses right on the camera. Everyone laughed, including the cameraman, who had to wipe off the smudges we left on his camera lens.

"Hey, Rootbeer," Edward said. "Remember the 'cool' guy from our previous visit? Here he comes."

He walked right up to Gloria and asked if he could take me for a walk. This time, he wasn't wearing his cap and didn't try to act cool. He started out happy and friendly like he was at the end of our walk last time. Standing tall but relaxed, he chatted away with Gloria. A couple of times, he stopped to ask people to take pictures of us together.

Afterward, his teacher whispered to Lilly, "That student had trouble paying attention in class today. He just kept watching the clock, waiting for the minis to come. I thought it was wonderful that he felt such a connection with the little horses."

Toward the end of the visit, everyone gathered in the central courtyard. Solo, Balonee, Cody, the bunny, and the snake were there, too.

"Calvin Klein is the perfect name for this bunny," one reporter said. "The students love petting him. One girl told me that Calvin feels like velvet. She said he's even softer than Solo, and Solo is like silk! I can't get over how the students respond to these animals."

"Velvet must be something special, Rootbeer. Do you think we could touch Calvin?"

"Robin might be afraid we'd scare him," I said. "Let's see if we can see him through the windows in his container. It looks to me like he stays in another kind of corral, but he sure is all snuggly in his soft blankets."

"I'd like to see the snake. I wish someone would say his name," Edward said. "Maybe next time."

The media snapped pictures, and people clapped and cheered at my rearing trick. I kept on rearing even when Lilly didn't ask me to. "Nice try, Rootbeer," she said sweetly. "Remember you only get a carrot when I ask you to rear."

Hey, you can't blame a guy for trying. I could tell Lilly thought it was funny.

Even though we liked our new experience, the day wore us out. We both slept lying down part of that night.

Over the next several days, people came up to Lilly and told her that they had heard, seen, and read all about us. They made statements like, "I saw Edward and Rootbeer on the TV news," or "I heard a story about the minis on the radio," or "I read all about your mini stars in the newspaper."

"Sounds like you guys are all over the news," Kiefer said across the aisle. "You'll be giving hoof autographs soon."

Lilly came into our corral, gave us great scratches, and said, "You two are a hit wherever you go.

"Principal Chuck called to say everyone at the school loved hearing and seeing the news and reading the newspaper articles. He framed copies of all the articles, hung them on his famous PET office wall, and thanked us over and over for coming.

"Then Robin called, saying that people from other schools and care places saw the media reports and asked if we can visit them too. You two are going to be busy.

"You gentlemen make me proud, but even better, you make me smile. I love you!"

Edward and I nickered happily to each other, to Kiefer, and to Lilly.

Once we were alone munching our extra carrot treats, Edward said, "New places and people don't scare us anymore, do they, Rootbeer?"

"Nope," I agreed. "Just think, Edward. We made friends with animals that aren't anything like us. We know people of all ages who love being around animals. We have the best job ever."

"You'll laugh, Rootbeer, but I think smiles are even better than carrots."

Lilly stuck her head around the corner. "Well, gentlemen, I wanted to say goodnight again and give you and Kiefer more carrots. I have a feeling our adventures have just started!"

When we heard Lilly drive off, I said to Edward with a twinkle in my eye, "If smiles are better, why don't you push your carrots over to me?"

Edward acted like he didn't hear a word I said.

Whoa!

"Did you hear Lilly? We're in for another new and unusual experience," I said. "This one sounds entirely different from all the rest."

"Yes, I heard a little of what she said to someone on the phone. You seem unsure," Edward said. "What do you think a National Horse Show is and what will we do there?"

"All I know is the same thing you heard Lilly say on that telephone call. It's something about people seeing horses of various sizes, and that we'll be with two other horses, one big and the other medium.

"It definitely will be different. Hold on, here come Lilly and Janet. Maybe they'll talk about it."

"Susann said there is an area where people who come to the horse show to see competitions will have an opportunity to be up-close and personal with horses," Lilly explained. "She wants to give them a chance to touch a horse."

"Do you think all the crowds will make the minis nervous?" Janet asked.

"I hope they've had enough training and experiences to be fine with all of it, but we'll watch carefully to be sure. Many people who come have horses and they bring children and friends who don't. Some have never been near a horse and Susann wants them, especially kids, to have that opportunity. Her goal is to educate and entice people into the world of horses."

"This will be fun for us," Janet said. "I hope it is for Rootbeer and Edward, too. The fairgrounds are beautiful. As I recall from last year, the competitions take place over three weeks. The first week is dedicated to Western riding, the next week to dressage, and the final to jumping. Remember that amazing finale last year with horses that cleared jumps five feet high? Wow! Will we be there all three weeks?"

"Only on the three Saturdays," Lilly said. "Can you do all three?"

"Of course! There's nowhere else I'd rather be."

"Thanks, Janet. And last year? I sure do remember it," Lilly said. "The horse and rider were judged by how many of the ten jumps they could get across without knocking down any poles—and in the fastest time. I think I held my breath the whole competition.

"Thanks so much for agreeing to go all three Saturdays. We'll arrive in the early afternoon, and since each Saturday night ends with a big show of the featured riding for that week, we'll stay until the show starts."

"You're welcome. I'm delighted to help. Being around these two great minis always makes me happy. We'll have a blast," Janet said.

"Okay, let's meet here tomorrow about noon to get our gentlemen glowing so we can leave an hour later," Lilly said. "I'll have the rig all set to go."

The next morning, the routine was the same as before every other trip. We played and ate, and when Janet arrived, the two of them brushed us and led us to the trailer. The hay bag hung in its usual spot and we hopped right in.

In no time at all, the rig slowed down and turned into a huge, concrete parking lot lined with thousands of white-striped parking places. A wide busy street lay beyond that.

At the fairgrounds entrance, the gate guard peaked through the trailer slats and asked, "Where are you taking these two handsome horses?"

Lilly explained why we were there and the guard directed her to another gate past a fancy entrance to a huge arena.

At that gate, another guard showed Lilly where to park. While Lilly went to find out where we'd be for the afternoon, Janet told us what she saw.

"Boys, there's a stage where a band will play music for people to enjoy. I want to warn you that the music might be very loud." Our ears twitched at that, but she continued her description. "All around the stage are various food booths. People can get almost any kind of food and drink they want, sit on benches, and listen to the music."

"Ah, food. That will make the music okay," Edward said. I wasn't so sure.

"Other booths have colorful displays where people can buy horse equipment like saddles, bridles, blankets, and halters. Still more booths have riding clothes and horse-themed toys. Even with all of these attractions, I'll bet you two are the stars of the day!"

When Lilly returned, she and Janet haltered and walked us through the area which was exactly as Janet described.

"It's already bustling with activity and most of the visitors haven't arrived," Lilly said.

"This is going to be hectic," Edward said. "Will you be okay?"

"Don't worry, I'll be fine," I said without much conviction.

"Welcome, gentlemen. I am so glad you're here," called Susann.

"Hi there," Lilly said. "Janet, gentlemen, this is Susann who you may have seen at our ranch. She organized this wonderful exhibit. You'll love the spot she set up for you."

Our corral was one of four, loaded with shavings, a

bucket of water, and best of all, piles of hay.

"Before the gates open to let in the visitors and before you're in your special corral, let's meet the other two horses who each have their own corral," Lilly said.

"This white horse is Billy, a Welsh Pony. The large horse is a Peruvian. His name is Echo," Susann said. "The four of you will be sharing the spotlight for three Saturdays, so let's meet." Susann introduced us to each other and let us get closer and closer.

"Let's touch noses with them, Rootbeer," Edward suggested. "They are very handsome."

"They are. I love Echo's shiny red chestnut color," I said.

Lilly stepped forward and reminded us to take it nice and easy, but we were already friendly and touched noses.

"What's this corral for?" Janet asked. The fourth corral had four bales of hay each topped with a saddle.

"My reason for this corral is so kids have the opportunity to feel what it's like to sit in a saddle," Susann answered.

"Great idea," Janet said.

"Hey guys," Lilly said pointing to a sign. "Look at what Susann had made just for you. It says, '73rd Horse Show, Miniature Horses, Rootbeer 15 years old, Edward 16 years old.' She made similar signs for the other two horses. How special."

Edward and I just celebrated our birthdays and now we are 16 and 15 years old. Lilly had a little birthday party and gave us and Kiefer extra carrots. She also made a carrot cake for her friends at the ranch. We wished she'd given us a taste of the cake, but she said it was people food.

Once the fairgrounds opened for the horse show, tons of people came in. Everyone was happy and seemed surprised to see us and the other horses. I don't think they expected to have an opportunity to get so close. Just like everywhere we go, some people were confident around us and others seemed unsure about touching us. The whole afternoon we felt like rock stars with people taking photo after photo, and of course, there were happy smiles wherever we looked.

When the sun went down, Edward said, "Can't beat a day like this, can we, Rootbeer? People petting us, asking questions about us, taking our pictures, and all we have to do is look up at them and then eat some more."

"You're right. This was a good day for sure, but a little tiring too. We haven't had our usual quiet time or a chance to run and play. It's starting to get dark and Lilly said we'd leave when everyone goes inside the arena for the show. She called the show 'The Night of the Horse.'"

"Every night should be night of the horse," Edward said.

Just as Edward started to say he was ready to be home, we heard singing.

"That's our National Anthem," Lilly said, "which someone with a beautiful voice sings before the main show starts. It's our signal to head home, gentlemen. We've had a big day."

That was music to my ears. The day was tiring and I was ready for the gentle sounds of our home, including a little play time.

When we neared our trailer, I said, "It looks like you will go in first, Edward. I'll be here with Janet while Lilly puts on your fly mask."

Edward hopped into the trailer. Thinking Edward was securely in and eating, Lilly turned to reach for my lead rope. That's when things got crazy!

Edward leaped out and ran. Startled, I turned to see what he was doing. I must have jerked hard, because my halter fell off and I went running after him. Feeling the explosion of pent up energy, we galloped through the fairgrounds.

I caught up to Edward and together we raced faster and faster. We didn't know anything about the fairgrounds, but soon discovered how huge it was. It seemed endless. We galloped at top speed through a narrow parking lot, past two-story buildings that looked like places where people live, past exhibition halls, through open spaces, and into more parking lots.

Finally, we reached a place where we had to turn left or right. I looked back and saw Lilly running after us with Janet not far behind her. They looked frantic, but we kept running for all we were worth.

"We need to go this way," Edward said, pushing me to the right.

I had no idea why, but I could see that the other way led to the giant parking lot and wide street. Off we ran, although I began to feel guilty for not listening to Lilly calling us, sounding upset and scared. The joy of running overrode my guilt, especially after being cooped up in the stall getting attention all day.

"Edward," I finally said, "we need to stop."

"Not yet. Someone over here needs us." He yelled back at me, "Come on!"

After we made another right turn we were in a big parking area where two young girls and two ladies were standing and talking.

They all looked shocked when they saw us charging

toward them, but I guess it would be surprising to see two little horses running loose, followed by two women running behind calling our names. All around, men were driving carts down the road, zipping in between parked cars and trucks.

Then I spotted what Edward had meant when he said someone needed us. A little boy was running madly around, whinnying like he was a horse, prancing and jumping pretend jumps.

"Come on, Rootbeer," Edward said. "That boy is not watching where he's going, and I don't think the men driving the carts see him. We have to head him off or he'll be hurt."

The two women were engrossed in their conversation and hadn't noticed the child was in danger. Sure enough, the little boy was totally distracted by his game imitating a wild horse and hadn't paid attention to where he was going. He didn't notice the big cart coming toward him. The driver and his passenger were chatting and laughing, not looking ahead. I'm sure they didn't expect to see a kid playing horse, and certainly not two galloping miniature horses.

We ran full steam toward the boy and the cart. I got there before Edward and leaped up into the air hoping the driver would see me. The driver looked up in shock and slammed on the brakes. At that moment Edward gave the boy a head butt so hard, it sent the 'little wild horse' sprawling, but safely away from the cart.

The driver who had swerved and then screeched to a stop jumped from the cart and hurried over to where the boy lay. Closely behind them were the two ladies and two little girls— all frightened.

The little boy stood up shakily, crying, and looking at the bloody scrapes and scratches on his leg.

Then Lilly and Janet came racing up to us, completely out of breath, looking equally frightened.

"I only saw the very end, but I think Edward knocked the boy down. Is he your son?" Lilly asked, between gasps. "I am so sorry."

"Yes, he is, but don't apologize," his mom said. "I saw the whole thing and these two little horses saved my son from being hit by the cart. They are heroes!!! The spotted one leaped in front of the cart as if to warn the cart driver. Then the little black horse pushed my boy clear of the cart. I'm afraid the bigger horse might be hurt, because I saw the cart clip his leg."

By now Janet had haltered us and stood off to the side with us, waiting for Lilly to come over.

The moms and kids kept repeating, "These two little horses are amazing. They are heroes!" The little boy agreed, and despite being hurt and crying, he smiled at us.

"Are you badly hurt?" Lilly asked the boy. "I want to check on you and then I'll see about Rootbeer's leg."

"No," he said, trying to stop crying and wiping the tears from his cheeks. "I was playing horsey and wasn't watching where I was going. I didn't see the cart. The scratches hurt a little, but I'm excited to see these horses. It's like playing horsey made horses come alive."

Lilly walked over to Janet and us, squatted down and examined my leg.

"There's some blood, but it looks like a surface cut," Janet said. "What do you think?"

"I agree it's surface. Are you okay, Rootbeer?" Lilly asked in a soft, gentle voice. "We can clean it out and put ointment on it when we get back to the barn.

"Well," Lilly continued, "now that the excitement is over, gentlemen, let's go back to the group and make some introductions."

Everyone met everyone and then all three kids took turns hugging us, telling us how smart and brave we are, and how much they love us. They asked if they could have their pictures taken with us, so the women took lots of pictures and did that adult happy-teary thing. Once again, the boy's mom thanked Lilly.

"I don't know how your horses knew, but somehow they came at the right time. I hate to think how badly my son could have been hurt. We'll never forget our introduction to miniature horses!"

"We won't forget you either," Lilly assured her. "Horses are very sensitive and have powerful instincts. They proved that today—fortunately."

"Well now, gentlemen, it really is time for us to go. I think that's enough drama for today. Maybe for a long, long time," Lilly said tiredly.

Edward and I hung our heads, feeling bad for putting her and Janet through that trouble.

"How about we walk back to the trailer," Janet said with a small smile and a sigh. "I'm relieved but exhausted.

You must be too, Lilly."

On our way back to the trailer, Edward said, "Wow, we ran a long way! No wonder everyone is tired out."

Before we got to the trailer, Lilly stopped and turned to face us.

"You did a very good deed, but I am disappointed you took off like that and didn't stop when I called you. It scared us, right Janet?"

"Absolutely," she said. "You could have gotten lost or badly hurt. If you'd turned left and gone into the parking lot and street, who knows what could have happened. Besides, it's not good for my heart to be so frightened!"

Both Lilly and Janet leaned down to give us scratches, which we really didn't deserve.

"Please, don't ever, ever, ever do that again," Lilly said.

"You know Lilly is right," I said to Edward when we were back in the trailer. "That was not good behavior. In fact, it was terrible behavior. Why did you jump out?"

"Who knows, Rootbeer. I was full of energy after standing all day and I didn't think. I just leaped and ran. Why did your halter fall off?"

"Who knows is my answer too," I said. "That never

happened before either. I'll bet Lilly and Janet make sure our halters are on extra tight from now on.

"Bad as it was, the running did feel good, but I have to admit I am ready to be home," I said in the midst of a giant yawn.

"Do you think you'll be able to sleep?" Edward asked. "Your leg is bloody and looks sore. Does it hurt?"

"A little but Lilly and Janet will clean it. I'll be fine, just like the little boy will be with his scratches. The cart driver hit me because I got there first which slowed him, but you're the one that pushed the boy out of the way."

"Teamwork, my brother," Edward said. "I know I shouldn't feel proud, but I have to admit that was my all-time best head butt!"

He looked over at me and added, "So, maybe it IS okay to head butt."

As I glanced at him, I saw his twinkling eyes and impish expression.

"Maybe, just maybe...but only ONCE in a great while, Edward!"

After another day of "firsts," I wondered what could possibly happen next.

I looked at Edward to ask him, but he had his nose buried in the hay bag, picking out the sweetest morsels.

The End

About the Author Rene Townsend

Rene pictured with the real-life minis, Rootbeer (left) and Edward.

A life-long animal lover, Rene grew up with cats, dogs, and later bunnies. Finally, she got the beautiful horses of her dreams, Oz and Kiefer. Then, falling in love with two miniature horses who needed a new home, she added them to her herd, changing her life—and the lives of others—in unexpected ways. Rene was a school teacher, principal, district superintendent, university lecturer, partner in a superintendent search firm, and education outreach director for Central America through a San Diego charity. Her passion for education continues with this book about the adventures of Rootbeer & Edward, smile ambassadors who live a life of learning, playing and serving others and who, every day, make Rene laugh.

About the Illustrator Gina Dodge

Gina is a maker of all sorts. At a young age she proclaimed, "I want to be an artist or a singer." Art currently dominates her life. Her medium of choice usually falls into the realm of painting, but she is infatuated with creating anything she can get her hands on. She enjoys expressing her keen sense of humor through her work and inspiring others just by being herself.

Gina Dodge

CPSIA information can be obtained
at www.ICGtesting.com
Printed in the USA
FSHW011639141118
53767FS